I0691995

COLLEEN O'MERRY
Dominatrix to the Stars

First Edition

Published by The Nazca Plains Corporation
Las Vegas, Nevada
2010

ISBN: 978-1-935509-97-4
Ebook: 978-1-61098-012-8

Published by

The Nazca Plains Corporation ®
4640 Paradise Rd, Suite 141
Las Vegas NV 89109-8000

PUBLISHER'S NOTE
Colleen O'Merry is a work of fiction created wholly by *Tim Desmondes'* imagination. All characters are fictional and any resemblance to any persons living or deceased is purely by accident. No portion of this book reflects any real person or events.

Cover Photo, Lev Dolgatshjov
Art Director, Blake Stephens

DEDICATION

An actor by the name of Flynn used to tell yarns about an Irish lass who dug bearing pain and inflicting it as well.

She was said to have made a good living from pleasing both the sadists and masochist who were part of the Hollywood scene in Hollywood's Golden Years.

So, whether she existed in the real or in the virtual world, I have brought her back to dwell in the following pages.

This book is dedicated to Colleen O'Merry, the subject of Mister Flynn's anecdotes.

God bless her.

Tim Desmondes

COLLEEN O'MERRY
Dominatrix to the Stars

First Edition

Tim Desmondes

CONTENTS

CHAPTER ONE

Irish Beginnings

Well, hello there.

My name is Colleen and I'm Irish.

I imagine you could guess that from my accent and my name anyway. Couldn't you?

Colleen is an old Irish name and it means "pure" in our Gaelic tongue.

But pure am I not.

Because I was a bad girl.

I'm an adult now, so I'm not a little girl any more. But bad I am. And I need and deserve to be punished.

My daddy enjoyed giving me the spankings I deserved when I was a tot.

I could tell that it pleased him to punish me because of the tent he made in his pants when he did it.

He always took me over his knee and his thing rose up in his pants and quivered. I asked him about that and he told me that only showed that he loved me very much. And that it was an indication that he loved me enough to teach me a good lesson not to do bad, wicked things ever again.

The way it happened was always the same.

Mommy or Daddy would find me playing an innocent game with a playmate. Most of the time, they chose to guess that I had done some evil deed. Although such was never the case I always agreed that I had done so.

I had learned the kinds of things Daddy and Mommy liked to hear and I confessed to one of those things each time they "caught" me.

Then Daddy would take me into his den and say:

"Colleen, you have been a naughty little girl, haven't you?"

And whether I had actually been caught doing something bad or not, I always said, "Yes, Daddy."

Then he said, "Confess to me what it was you did."

And I'd have to guess what sinful thing they thought I'd been doing and confess to it.

Then Daddy always said, "What do you say now, Colleen?"

And I would always answer, "I am a wicked child, and I'm sorry. I need to be punished."

Even though I knew I had not done anything wrong, that's what my parents wanted me to say.

Then I could tell Daddy was pleased with my answer because of that tenting thing he did in his pants. After his tenting he always beat me.

Oh, my goodness how Daddy could wallop.

He always began with his bare hand on my bare bottom. He spanked me until both his palm and my ass were bright red and stinging.

Then, because his hand got sore, he picked up his wooden paddle and spanked me until I was crying real hard.

Then, I got off his lap, bent over and grabbed my ankles with my bare butt exposed as he picked up either his bamboo cane, his riding crop, or his razor strop and laid into me until he raised welts on me or even drew blood.

When Daddy said I could let go of my ankles and stand up he told me:

"That hurt me more than it did you, Colleen. Let that be a lesson to you. Never do (whatever I had confessed to) again."

And I answered through my sobs, wailings and tears, "I won't Daddy."

I'm sure both of us knew I was lying. But that was the game we played.

And I knew that he really loved me. Because after my beating, he still had that throbbing thing going on inside his pants.

Those spankings that I had received regularly, several times every week, as far back as I could remember, came to a stop one day.

I'll tell you about it.

It was on a beautiful spring day.

Timmy O'Shaunessy and I were playing in our garage. We were playing our favorite game, patty-cake.

Mommy, like always, said she suspected something naughty was going on and was listening outside the door to what we were doing.

She came bursting though the door and discovered that we were playing pattycake, real nice.

"Just you wait 'til your father comes home," Mommy warned me.

But, as it happened, Daddy did not come home that evening.

He never ever came back home.

He and Mrs. Dugan went off to Mullinahone to play house and I never saw him again.

So he never got a chance to ask me:

"Colleen, you have been a naughty girl, haven't you?"

And I never got a chance to confess to him what he wanted me to say.

And he never had a chance to show me how much he loved me by chastising and punishing me.

And, O my God! How I miss my daddy.

Well, after daddy went off to play house, Mommy and I went to live with Aunt Margaret. Actually, she's my great-aunt because she's Mommy's real aunt.

Aunt Margaret is rich and Mommy and I were real poor after Daddy left.

And Aunt Margaret is strict. Real strict. She was always talking about Hell and sin, and wickedness and damnation, and the Last Days, and all that. And if she had ever heard about the bad things I was always doing or that Mommy liked to imagine me doing, Aunt Margaret would have tossed both Mommy and me right out of her home and onto the street on our asses without a penny to our name.

So, as far as Aunt Margaret was concerned, I was as pure a little darling as my name, Colleen, suggested.

Last year, when I turned eighteen, Aunt Margaret told me it was high time I left her home and began supporting myself like any good Christian young lady should.

I knew I would have to get my job search underway immediately. Aunt Margaret is not the most patient person in the world. If she had determined that there was some kind of moral imperative for me to get myself gainfully employed, I had better get with it while I still had free room and board at her home.

I had not really given any previous thought to the matter. What was I qualified to do out in that ugly world of work?

The thing I was best at in school was swimming. My school was one that had a pool and a water sports program.

Aunt Margaret had been of the opinion that athletics was just the thing young people should be engaged in. That exercise was godly since the body is the container of the soul and all that. So she encouraged my swimming.

I happen to have been blessed with a strong body with fine reflexes. I swim like a dolphin and, since our school competed in water sorts with many schools in southern County Cork, I was the captain of the girls' swim team for two years.

One of the schools we had competed with while I was captain of my team was Ballycormac Academy.

I got wind that the coach of the girls' team there had resigned her job. So I called the school to see if they were interviewing for the position.

I was delighted that Headmaster McCarthy wanted to interview me.

I was given a date and time to meet with him.

When I got to Ballycormac and the academy, I was ushered into the headmaster's office.

I was met by a tall distinguished looking white-haired gentleman who had set two identical looking chairs facing each other in the center of his office. He bade me sit in one and sat himself in the other facing me about two yards distance away.

We smiled cheerfully at each other. I was happy to see that this interview would be in a friendly mode rather than a grim one.

He informed me that he recognized me.

It turned out that he was a great fan of his girls' swim team and had admired my form when my team came to Ballycormac to compete.

My "form?" Hmmm.

He made comments not lacking in innuendo about my "breast stroke" and my "fluttering leg work."

He punctuated his references with obvious ogling of the relevant appendages of my lissome body.

I could tell I was making a good impression on him by the jig being danced by the organ behind the fly of his trousers.

He mentioned that he, himself, was not adverse to "paddling" around in the pool.

"Would you care to see my paddle?" he asked archly.

I enthusiastically assured him that nothing would give me more pleasure.

He asked me if I was of good moral character.

I told him that I sometimes did things that were considered naughty but that my father had taught me that there were painful consequences for my actions. It was clear to me that was what he wanted to hear.

In short, before the interview was over, I had confessed to doing things I was ashamed of and would welcome chastisement from a father figure.

Headmaster McCarthy arose, his ascent somewhat hampered by the bulge in his pants. He proceeded to his desk, removed a paddle which he kept there "for the purpose of maintaining discipline at the academy."

And before I left his office, my bare ass was tingling very painfully and I had landed the job as coach of the Ballycormac Academy's girls' swim team.

When I returned home that evening I could hardly wait to get to my room and into bed. The paddling I had received in Ballycormac had gotten me so hot I needed to come.

Now, back in my bed, nude, with my legs spread wide, my naughty fingers assaulted my gash, one dancing tippy-toe on my clit and the other running up and down my love channel.

Ahh! I had landed a job, I had come, and life was good!

Within a few weeks I took leave of my mother and my aunt and headed west to assume my responsibilities in the wide new world of employment.

The coaching job turned out to be a true delight. The girls welcomed me and were quite receptive to all my coaching directions. And when our team got into competition, we more than held our own.

Every couple of weeks or so I reported to Headmaster McCarthy to confess to some imagined naughty thing I had done for which I needed correction. The transgressions never, ever, had anything to do with any activity I had engaged in with anyone at the school or within the community of Ballycormac. I knew full well that I would be fired on the spot if I did anything that might bring repercussions from within the community.

At the end of my team's practice one day, I remained in the pool room after all my students had left.

When I was sure the gym was empty and the doors locked, I lay on the diving board to relax. I had often found that a nice fluffing off of my cunt was the perfect recreation once the workday was over.

I removed my bathing suit, my back flush with the board, and embraced my golden orbs.

I squeezed, I rubbed, I massaged.

My fingers worked slowly but determinedly to engage the tender little dotted bumps of the aureoles that encircle my nipples.

Ah, how relaxing it was when my fingertips pranced pleasantly around those engorging nipples.

When I had succumbed to the pulsing sensations at my bosom, I tweaked the nipples themselves and pulled at them until they budded forth with exuberance.

At that point I left one hand to nipple-hop back and forth as my other hand traced arabesques down to explore my navel for a while. Then it made a leisurely brushing action over my beaver.

Ah, how sweet it was. There was no rush. My koozie was becoming delightfully damp, but was content to await the soft caresses it knew would be attending it soon.

My nipples began to demand brisker activity from the fingers and thumb of my left hand. I tweaked and plucked at them until they obediently pebbled.

I pulled my knees up and spread them wide apart, opening my pussy to breathe in the heavy damp air of the pool room.

My nipples protested when I removed my left hand from its ministrations there to rest on my outstretched left knee. Simultaneously my right hand found itself resting on its corresponding knee.

Somehow, without my consciously willing it, my fingers glided slowly and resolutely from my knees to tickle their way down the soft, sensitive skin of my inner thighs.

I slowly and sensuously sucked each index finger as though giving head to a mini-dong. Although my crack was already redolently damp, I wanted my probing fingers to get even more slippery.

I approached my slit slowly, oh, ever so stealthily, making myself grow desperate for the attack on my pussy-lips. Then, those slippery fingers made a sudden attack, separating those lips and opening the hole to the ceiling above.

Up and down, up and down my fingers massaged those welcoming labia. Ahhh! Yes!!!

Would I let one of those spit-lubricated mini-phalli enter my treasure garden and finger-fuck me to orgasm? Or was it time to lift the hood that still hid my clit?

An excruciating decision

I knew the cute little bud in there was palpitating and screaming for a gentle massage and a love pinch.

Would I torture it and make it wait? Or assault it to its satisfaction?

How about shoving my right finger into my cunt while the other finger sought to further uncover the boy in the boat?

While I was pondering that move, I glanced up toward the high dive, and what did I see?

Jamie O'Doul. That's what I saw. Or should I say whom I saw?

Jamie O'Doul, the golden boy of the student body. A graduating senior.

And what a sight he was. Hair as blond as an angel. A face to rival any movie star. A torso with pects and abs sculpted like a Greek statue. The eldest son of Carlisle O'Doul, the richest man in the county.

Now what do you think that paragon of young manliness was doing up there on the platform?

He was seated, bending over, his legs dangling down towards the pool, and staring directly at me, watching me pleasure myself.

And most eye-catching of all, he was jacking off into the pool.

When our eyes met, he spoke softly but firmly to me.

"Do not come, yet, coach. It'd be cooler by far if we were to bring each other off."

I immediately removed my hands from my erogenous zones in surprise as well as in anticipation of what he was proposing.

He hoisted himself up onto his feet, lifted his arms above his head, and performed a perfect swan dive into the pool.

When he surfaced and climbed out of the pool next to me, I noticed that his hardon had softened somewhat due to effect of his dive.

I knew neither of us would need to wait long for it to revive.

Without asking, he bent over me and kissed me on the mouth.

The passion of his kiss, as our tongues met each other in a slurpy, passionate exchange, caused me to drip an abundance of nectar down onto the diving board from between my legs.

When we withdrew from the clinch, he rose up on his knees and I saw that his beautiful youthful prick was standing at awesome attention.

"Don't move," he commanded. "The situation suggests an old-fashioned sixty-nine to bring us each to a perfect consummation."

He maneuvered himself into position above me, his adorable mouth aimed towards my snatch and his brave peckerhead staring at my drooling mouth.

He lowered himself down toward me, adroitly slipping the bulbous crown of his cock into my waiting lips as his tongue made contact with my gaping hole.

Talk about gobbling! The sounds of our licking, sucking, and probing filled that pool room with a symphony of ecstatic harmonies.

Our epiphany was so fantastic my whole body felt shattered.

Jamie backed off the board onto the side of the pool. I slithered behind him.

There we stood, taking in the sight of each other's satisfied body, and we burst out laughing.

But wait! There was another burst. A quick burst of light. A flash.

O my God! It was the flash bulb of a camera.

And guess who had just snapped a very revealing picture of the girls' swim teacher and coach and the big boy on campus?

Headmaster McCarthy, camera in hand and scowl on face was glaring at us.

He stared straight at Jamie.

"You, Jamie O'Doul. Get your clothes back on, and get out of here fast. And never mention this incident to a single soul. And that includes your father who could very well disinherit you for shaming the family name."

Before I could blink an eye, Jamie had scooted into the boys' locker room.

"And you, Miss Colleen O'Merry. Get yourself properly dressed and come to my office as soon as you can make it.

"You have been a very naughty girl. You need to confess to me what you have done here. And ask to be punished for your heinous seduction of an innocent youth."

The only words I had for my employer at that moment were these: "Yes, Sir."

The scowl on his face morphed into a sneer.

And without a further word he marched as though in triumph out the door.

As rapidly as I could get to my room in the faculty quarters I sought out apparel that I felt would appeal to the headmaster in his guise as discipliner of naughty instructresses.

I seldom wear thong underwear. But remembering the tingles in my butt cheeks from Headmaster McCarthy's paddle, I believed he would look favorably upon my appearing in a thong.

Over the thong I put on my short-short skirt that had a tendency to reveal the lower moons of my ass when I leaned forward at all. I knew he would like that.

I did not put on a brassiere, of course. And for a top I had a nearly translucent silk blouse that clung revealingly to my breasts.

I decided against stockings and slipped into my stiletto heels barefoot.

I headed out the door proceeding to my boss' office for whatever correction he was likely to administer.

And I felt quite sure the discipline would involve me leaning across his boner enhanced lap with my bare cheeks revealed to the ceiling.

And that I would leave his office with a deliciously tingly red ass that would get my pussy watering, ready for a leisurely fluffing off when I got back to my room.

Such was my anticipation.

When I got to Professor McCarthy's door in the administration wing of the school I knocked gently.

The door did not open immediately. He kept me waiting outside in the hallway. I knew he was relaxing in his office relishing the thought that I would be trembling outside in terror of his paddle.

I felt so smug. Paddle? Bring it on! My koozie dampened up delightfully at the thought.

As I waited I pinched my nipples so they would perk up for my employer's visual pleasure.

When the door opened, the headmaster stepped back so I could enter his office.

"Close the door behind you and bolt it, Slut!" he demanded with a scowl on his face.

I did as ordered and stood before him, arching my back so my boobs would provide some visual entertainment for my inquisitor.

We looked each other up and down. His eyes lingered on my aroused pointing boobs.

His most notable feature, at which I stared feigning awed admiration, was the hardon jiggling away within his pants.

"What are you here for?" he demanded.

"I have been remiss in my duties as an instructress and am here to receive chastisement," I answered.

I had learned very young the kind of answer expected of a miscreant like me.

He stepped up to me and gave me a very sharp slap to the face. My eyes lost temporary focus and my ears rang.

Jesus! That was a good one!

"At the end of every answer to me, do not forget to state 'Sir.' If you should ever forget, you can expect a similar reminder. Do you understand?"

"Yes, Sir," I shot back crisply. I am a fast learner.

"Now," he said. "Let us begin again. Why are you here?"

"I misbehaved with one of the school's students and am here to receive chastisement..."

He prepared to administer a slap to my other cheek but I managed to get in the next word before he could administer the sharp reprimand.

"..., Sir.!"

"Confess what reprehensible thing you did to or with said student."

"I seduced him, Sir."

"More specifically, what act did you demean him with, Whore?"

"I sucked his cock, Sir."

"And how did the young man reciprocate, Harlot?"

"By doing a sixty-nine with me, Sir."

"Describe!"

"While I was sucking his cock, he was eating my snatch, Sir."

"That is a grievous situation," he informed me.

"I agree, Sir. And I am very repentant. So I seek punishment for my foul depravity."

I thought I was playing my part pretty well and hoped we'd get to the spanking with the paddle pretty soon.

But he surprised me.

"An abomination of such magnitude requires extreme measures," he informed me.

"Do you see that door at the far end of this office?"

The door he was referring to was so obvious that his question was somewhat ridiculous, I thought. But I answered it seriously.

"Yes, I do."

Slap!

Oh my God! That *really* stung bad. He'd slapped my other cheek and had practically knocked me off my feet.

"Sir!" I belted out.

"Enter the door to that chamber and remove all your clothing, you filthy bitch. Be sure to fold everything neatly in a corner. Do *not* close the door behind you."

Chamber? Remove my...? What the Hell was this all about?

But I marched smartly into the "chamber" and I had happened to dress in clothes that could be taken off quite quickly and easily.

As I was undressing I heard the door to the "chamber" slam.

I turned around and damned if the old boy wasn't confronting me nude as a newborn babe.

He was as trim and well-muscled as Jamie of recent recollection.

And he sported a hardon of worthy proportions.

The sight made my pussy twitch.

I ventured a look around the room.

The only sobriquet that appeared to my mind at first from what I observed was "torture chamber." That description was quickly replaced by "chamber of horrors."

I had no idea what most of the furnishings in the room actually were. But I knew they had to be familiar articles in any well-stocked chamber of horrors.

"Tell me how sorry you are for what you have done," McCarthy ordered.

"Oh, very sorry, Sir," I answered abjectly.

"Then do you deem your punishment should be light or harsh?"

"Oh, harsh, Sir."

"Harsh or very harsh?"

I wondered how long this act would have to play out before he'd get around to paddling my ass.

"Very harsh, Sir. With a very big paddle....Sir."

Well, that made him laugh.

Not a kind, gentle chuckle. But a laugh that was wildly demonic.

He picked up a pair of leather-lined handcuffs from a stand and approached me with a threatening stride.

"Extend your wrists to me," he ordered.

Oh-oh! Rough stuff ahead?

I obeyed him immediately, of course. And he snapped those suckers onto my wrists "toot sweet."

"Go over to that red circle in the middle of the chamber, kneel down in it, and hold your manacled hands together in supplication," he demanded.

"Yes, Sir," I responded.

Now, for the first time, I really was repentant. I could not imagine what torture awaited me.

But I was quite sure it would not be pretty.

When my knees hit the cold hard floor my heart's palpitation began to flutter. I was quite aware that I would soon be in deep shit of some kind.

There I was, bare-assed on my knees, handcuffed with my hands held before my face in a prayerful pose. I must have looked like some kind of God damned saint. Or, better yet, a martyr.

I was facing a large iron holdfast around which a thick hemp rope was wound. The rope angled from it towards the ceiling to a point directly above my head.

While the headmaster was slowly unwrapping the rope from its hold, I craned my head and neck upward to try to see what the rope led to. When I glimpsed the spot, I saw that it led through a pulley affixed to the ceiling. And that there was a large metal hook dangling down aimed towards the crown of my head at the end of the rope.

Oh, oh! The sight raised goose bumps all over me.

When Headmaster McCarthy had the rope unwound from its pin he walked to the spot where I was kneeling and lowered that gruesome hook to a space just above my head.

"Raise your hands above your head, Slut," he ordered.

I did so with trepidation.

"Beg me to hoist you up."

I hesitated.

"Now!" he grunted.

"Please, Sir," I sobbed. "Hoist me up."

He hitched my handcuffs over the hook and began to pull on the rope.

My arms were pulled up until they were stretched tight. Then, he continued to pull, raising me toward the ceiling. I was pulled off my knees. Then farther until I was dangling with my toes just barely touching the cold floor.

The man's muscles bulged with the effort of hoisting me. Who would have thought he could be such a muscle-man?

My shoulder muscles! The strain on them was very painful. My arm sockets! I feared dislocation.

But beyond the discomfort and the pain, what I experienced most was the deep horror of helplessness. I had submitted myself to whatever devilish acts this obvious sadist might wish to inflict on me.

He left me dangling there, in pain and fear, as he marched arrogantly to a bench and removed an article.

As he proceeded back towards me he demonstrated that it was a scourge of some kind.

He snapped it in front of him as he walked.

I made out what it was. The scourge was made up of a handle from which hung three strands of studded suede leather. The whip was about three feet in length. I trembled at the sight.

"Tell me what a worthless bitch you are," McCarthy demanded.

"I am a worthless bitch, Sir," I obeyed.

"Tell me you deserve to be flogged."

"I deserve to be flogged…Sir."

No sooner had I asked him to whip me than he flicked that flogger, making excruciating welts across my stretched midriff.

I screamed from the pain where the studded straps cut into my sensitive skin. Those studs were a bitch.

Then, without further demanding that I beg to be punished, he circled my body, laying lashes on my belly, my back, my ass, and my legs.

With each cruel lash I could not hold back my shrieks and moans of pain.

Thankfully his aim was such that no blows had landed yet on my tits or mound.

When he had made a complete tour around my body, leaving red stinging welts wherever his whip had landed, he stood in front of me.

His face bore proof of the sheer delight he took in his ministration of discipline.

And his engorged dong gave testimony to the erotic pleasure his actions invoked in him.

"You are a hanging sack of shit!" he yelled at me.

"Tell me you are a hanging sack of shit!"

"I am a hanging sack of shit," I managed to say through my violent sobs.

I was greeted with a violent slap to my face.

"Sir!" I added.

Humiliation now joined the shame of my pain and submission.

He returned to the linchpin, grabbed the rope, hoisted me a few inches higher, and secured me there.

Up until then, if I strained, I could somewhat relieve the pain at my shoulders momentarily by pressing my toes down onto the floor.

His current action left me literally hanging "like a sack of shit" without even the moments of relief I formerly obtained by pressing down with my toes.

Now, he gave my body a twist and I spun around crazily. As I swung helplessly he slashed with painful precision at my tits, my mound, and my ass.

The pain became unbearable…until…

Until, inexplicably, the pain morphed into pleasure.

My cunt that had been aflame with burning pain blazed alive with a drenching wild passion such as I had never before experienced. My whiplashed nipples were protruding to an extent I would never ever have believed possible.

As I experienced that surge of passion, McCarthy stopped my body from its swinging around.

He pulled me toward him, clasped the back of my head, pressed his mouth on mine, and inserted his tongue into my oral cavity.

I could not resist reciprocating.

Our tongues enjoyed each other in a wild fury of fervent kissing.

The passion of our kiss outrivaled the mad smooching Jamie and I had enjoyed on the diving board less than an hour previous.

McCarthy broke off our kiss and drew my busting nipples to his lascivious lips.

I knew how extended the nubs of my nipples were.

But he tugged at them with such ferocity I feared they would disappear down his throat.

My nipples, that had been painful beyond imagination from the taste of the studded suede strands now gave me such ecstasy that I thought I might die.

When he had exhausted the pleasure my breasts had given him, he lowered the rope again, to where I was on my knees.

My arms were still kept uncomfortably extended upward, but the pressure on my joints was greatly relieved.

Helplessly, on bended knees, I was now face to face with his blue woodie.

His cock-helmet was a raging purple color. And it was throbbing in time with his heartbeats.

I spied precum on his cock-slit.

He loosened the rope a bit more, causing my mouth to slump down on his overly aroused dick.

I was mad to take that glorious apparition into my drooling mouth.

His need to come was as great as mine. So I sucked and licked that baby with frenzy and gusto until I released the jism that spurted from the depths of his balls into my mouth and thence down my aching throat into my gullet.

I longed madly for release. Not release from my bondage. But release from my pent up passion.

"Please, Master," I begged. "I have succumbed to you. And I have sucked you off. I beg you to make me come as well."

My tormentor-lover slapped me roundly first on one cheek then on the other.

"How dare you suggest I demean myself to do such a thing. I demand an apology immediately."

I did apologize abjectly.

He lowered the rope.

As my arms descended, the pain occasioned by the act of relaxation was excruciating.   My joints and muscles complained even as they experienced relief.

"Get yourself dressed and return to my office as soon as you can. I am not through with you yet," he said and threatened.

Not through with me? The man had tortured me, wracking my body. He had then drawn his pleasure from me sucking him off. What more can he possibly want?

I knew I would soon find out.

CHAPTER TWO

Across the Bounding Main

When I entered his office this time, both the headmaster and I were fully attired and as proper appearing as when I had entered before. That entry moment had been not more than an hour previous, but it felt like an entire lifetime ago.

My crotch was still fully aroused. The man, having cruelly and forcibly required me to submit, had also caused me to reach sublime heights. But he had not allowed me to reach my climax.

McCarthy sat comfortably behind his desk while I stood before him enveloped in carnal agony.

I was keenly aware that my unattended desperation for orgasm was part of the torture he was still inflicting on me.

Whatever was to happen next in that office, I fervently hoped it would be brief. Because I urgently needed to get back to my room and fluff myself off.

McCarthy addressed me sternly.

"Are you satisfied that you have received sufficient chastisement for your aberrant behavior with a student of this school, Colleen?" he asked.

"Yes, Sir," I answered. "Thank you, sir."

"And I assume that you know full well that your further presence at Ballycormac Academy would be most disruptive."

I understood that he was saying I was being fired.

I guessed that was what he had meant when he told me in the Chamber that he was not through with me yet.

But I was wrong. He had still to release his bombshell.

"As long as you remain in Ireland, Colleen, this academy is not safe from scandal, rumor or calumny."

Oh-oh! This sounded really serious.

"I'm afraid I do not understand what you are getting at, Sir," I replied in confusion.

"Let me make myself clear, Young Lady. Within the hour you will be driven to the Port of Wexford. You will board a vessel there which will take you abroad."

The surprised expression on my face induced him to expatiate.

"If you even think of resisting such deportation, I have the photograph I took of you standing in shocking nudity with a certain young student.

"Should you still remain in the British Isles tomorrow at this time, I will have a print of the picture taken personally to your Aunt Margaret and placed in her hands. Do you perceive what that would mean?"

The old bastard had done some real snooping into my background. I immediately knew that if Aunt Margaret saw a picture like that, which would thoroughly offend her sensibilities, she would disown me.

Worse, she would throw my mother out of her home into utter poverty and destitution.

The son of a bitch was blackmailing me. He had my ass over a barrel.

So I told him what I had to say submissively.

"Yes, Sir. I will go directly to my room and pack."

The final word of the man who had disciplined me, humiliated me, and, yes, tortured me to sublimity uttered his final word.

"Dismissed!"

I left the administrative offices in a stupor and headed for my quarters.

But when I got to my room, I did not begin to start packing immediately.

Instead, I got nude, lay down in bed, and spread my legs wide.

I kneaded my titties, lathed my cunt with my spit-drenched hand, tickled the nub of my clit to the point of no return, and came, and came, and came again.

Leaving a pool of my snatch-elixir on the sheets, I packed my suitcase with my sparse belongings.

I did not have to wait long for the knock on the door by the lackey who was there to drive me to Wexford and an unknown future…where?

————

The visitor at my door was a modest young man whose name I did not know. But he was one of the school janitors I had seen around campus.

He was rather diffident, standing there with his cap in hand.

"The headmaster told me you wished to ride to Wexford," he muttered.

Although such was not actually the case, I was hardly going to explain that going to the port was not my wish but Headmaster McCarthy's. So I simply nodded my head.

I started to pick up my baggage but the young man told me he would carry it for me and headed down the hall with a suitcase in each hand.

I closed the door to my room, leaving nothing behind but my cunt-juice on the sheets.

I sat next to the lad in the car. Neither of us said a word to each other during the hour-long drive.

When we got to Wexford he clearly knew his destination. He headed for the wharves and parked at a mooring. It was clear to me that the boat (it could not fairly be called a ship) we headed for was the vessel that was to deport me to my new destination.

I knew what the vessel was. It is what is called a tramp steamer. And the best that could be said for it was that it appeared to be in disreputable shape.

The boat, of course, had a name. And that name was emblazoned luridly on its side and stern: SUBMISSIVE MISS.

The connotation made me wince.

Or was the feeling a frisson of naughty anticipation?

A strapping man wearing a seaman's white cap was watching us as we approached.

He was shirtless and had the strong physique of a stevedore.

"Ahoy!" he shouted at us. "You, Boy! Is that the poontang Mac paid me to haul to New York?"

Mac, I figured out was McCarthy. Poontang, an American nasty word for cunt clearly referred to me. And New York turned out to be the destination the headmaster had chosen for me.

I had no choice. It was "all aboard" for me, Miss Poontang.

The driver who had brought me to the wharf left abruptly without so much as a "good-bye."

I stood before the captain eyeing him and with him rudely and openly looking me up and down with lust in his eyes.

"Cast off!" he shouted.

The order clearly did not apply to me. So I looked about to see whom he was addressing.

A tall, trim, shirtless sailor sprang out of the cabin door, jumped over the railing onto the quay, released the hawsers, jumped back on board, and we were launched.

The engines that had been clanking ever since I had arrived on board made a sputtering, whining sound and we were moving out onto the Saint George's Channel.

For better or worse, I was leaving my native Ireland behind me.

"I am Captain O'Sullivan," the captain told me. "But you are only to call me Master Captain or simply Master. If you address me otherwise you will be punished."

He called over to the lanky sailor who had just jumped on and off the boat.

"Bates! Avast! Come here!"

The lad hastened over to his captain and saluted.

"Bates," Captain O'Sullivan announced crisply. "This here is Miss Poontang. She's our passenger for this crossing to New York. What do you think?"

Bates was simply gorgeous. Tall, thin, tan and with sculptured chest and abdominal muscles a female could skim her fingers over all day long.

When he took me in with his roving eyes, I could not help but notice that his dick did a trick, greeting me joyfully from within his snow-white trousers.

"She'll do, Captain," the hunk replied with a wry grin. "She'll do."

And in return for Bates' dick trick, I was ashamed to admit to myself that my crotch dampened.

"Poontang," the captain addressed me. "This here fellow is my first mate. Guess how you are to address him?"

"I wouldn't know…Master Captain."

"Like me, he is to be addressed as Master. Master Bates or simply as Master."

"Master Bates!" I chuckled to myself. "He can master-bate me any time he wants."

The smirk on my face did not go unnoticed by the two men.

"There are two other members of our crew, Poontang," Master Captain continued. "Engineer Aiden and Cook Fu. You will meet them in due course. But they are to be addressed as Master as well. That will be Master A and Master Fu. You *shall* remember that, shan't you, Poontang?"

"Yes, Master," I replied.

I got the picture. It appeared that my cruise across the Atlantic would provide the kind of entertainment I had experienced in Ballycormac. And that the entertainment was meant more for the crew than for the passenger.

Master Captain began to walk towards the stern of the boat and I followed submissively behind him.

When we got aft, he stopped at a dinghy that was secured there on a lift.

Master pointed out to me that the tiny boat had a name, *Dependence*. I noticed that there were neither oars nor oarlocks in the craft and that a long thick rope was attached to its prow.

"Take off your clothes and get in your boat," the captain ordered gruffly.

I had learned submission well enough from Headmaster McCarthy to comply immediately.

"You may place your clothing in your dinghy," he allowed.

My dinghy?

"I hope you like your little boat, Poontang. It is named the good ship *Dependence.*

"Climb in!"

I obeyed his order.

"Bates," my master shouted.

Master Bates came bounding out of the cabin.

"I want you to take a ride in your little boatie, Cunt," my master told me.

He seized my waist and lifted me over the gunwale of the skiff and lowered me onto its seat.

"Lend a hand, Bates. Grab hold of the winch and lower the wench into the briny deep."

Imagine my surprise as the dingy was pulled up into the air, thrust out over the aft railing of the *Submissive Miss*, and lowered down into the ship's wake.

The rope that was fastened to the dinghy's prow extended up to the deck where the two masters were standing observing my reaction.

And there I was, in a dinky little rowboat devoid of oars, being pulled along by the boat on which I was being carried to America.

My heart was in my throat.

Was I to be cut free from the tramp steamer to languish and die?

I panicked.

Until I felt the rope pulling me and my boatie back towards the steamer.

The tiny craft was pulled up onto its support. Master Bates activated the winch. And, with great relief, I found my little *Dependence*, with me, its passenger, back on its perch on the steamer's stern.

"Tell me you enjoyed your little sea voyage, Whore," the captain demanded.

"I enjoyed my little sea voyage, Master."

"Good. Now get your sluttish body out of the damned dinghy. It's time you learned the ultimate punishment for disobedience."

I stepped out awkwardly, nude, with no help from the two husky men.

"Now, Poontang," my master informed me.

"You will be privileged to enjoy your little boat ride for an unspecified period of time every day, rain or shine, until we reach our destination. While you are bouncing over the waves, the crew and I will confer about whether you have been properly submissive to each of us.

"If the decision goes against you, I will personally sever the rope as you are riding the waves in your dinghy. Do you understand?"

Sever the rope? That would be a death sentence.

Set afloat on the Atlantic Ocean, I would be subject to tide, wind, weather, dehydration, starvation or drowning.

I resolved to be as obedient, submissive and abject as was humanly possibly. And possibly even beyond human endurance. Regardless of what devilish tasks those bastards might demand of me.

"I understand, Master," I told him.

"Good girl," he praised. "Now, pick up your clothes and follow me. It's time for chapel"

Chapel? What the fuck?

Master Bates had left the deck while Master Captain had been explaining about my fate should I be disobedient.

I followed my master, feeling as abject as I knew he wanted me to appear. I was right behind him as he entered the door to the steps leading below deck.

He led me to a door located partway down the lower-deck aisle.

"Leave your clothes outside the chapel door," he ordered.

I placed my bundle at the spot he pointed to.

"The chapel must be entered nude," he explained as he removed his trousers, underpants, shoes and sox.

He stood facing me with a hardon aimed at my startled, wide-open eyes.

My mouth filled with saliva, my nipples stiffened and a flood of moisture formed at my twat. That pecker of his was a lovely sight.

He opened the door, entered, and I followed.

The chapel was dimly lit by candles. There was a six-foot tall wooden cross at the far wall with an altar in front of it.

As conventional as the room was for a chapel, I had a feeling the "services" here were unlikely to be very godly.

Master Bates was already in the room, naked.

The man, stripped, in addition to the splendid torso I had already observed, was magnificently hung as well.

Next to him was Master Fu, the ship's cook. He was shorter than the other two men, and was quite as nude. He was a beautiful specimen of oriental male pulchritude.

I was being saluted by three throbbing male phalli that were being gently stroked by busily engaged fists.

I came close to drooling.

"Kneel before the cross," the captain ordered.

I dropped to my knees immediately.

Ouch! Tough on the bare knees.

"Poontang!" he announced. "Meet Master Fu. He is our *chef de cuisine*. But he is also talented in many other areas. Tell Master Fu you are pleased to be his slave."

"Master Fu. I am pleased to be your slave. Sir."

The captain condescendingly patted me on the head.

"Fu has brought you a nice iron torque to wear snuggly around your neck, you evil cunt. You will notice that it has a metal ring welded on. That ring is provided so we can attach leashes and other restraints to your lovely body. Ask Fu to install the torque around your neck."

"Master, Fu," I implored. "Please install the torque around my neck."

The device opened and closed exactly like a handcuff. Fu approached me with it opened, encircled my neck and snapped the damned thing closed.

God, it was heavy, tight, and uncomfortable. I did not relish wearing the heavy, clumsy thing around my dainty neck throughout the entire voyage. But what choice did I have?

"Master Fu was kind enough to bring along a nice pair of iron handcuffs to adorn your graceful wrists. You would like to wear them, would you not?"

"I would be honored to wear the iron cuffs," I assented.

I noticed that each of the cuffs Fu had in hand had a ring welded onto it, as did my torque.

After I was manacled, I was allowed to stand so my ankles could receive ringed cuffs to match my handcuffs.

"Now that you are properly adorned," my captain told me. "You may approach the altar and bend over it, feet on the floor, forehead to the top, arms extended and legs splayed."

I wasn't sure I liked that idea. But complying certainly beat being set adrift on a wide ocean. So I marched right up to the table that served as an altar and "assumed the position."

Bates grabbed one of my arms, extended it out to the side and fastened it to the altar's edge to an eyebolt by my cuff ring.

Fu then stretched my arm to its limit in the other direction and hooked me to the other end.

God! The devils had me stretched tight. My boobs were pressed down painfully onto the altar's surface.

The two masters came around behind me and stretched my legs apart as far as they could go without tearing me apart at the pussy.

And then, as I expected, my ankle rings were affixed to the base of the altar. Master Captain now took over.

"How do you like it there, Poontang?" he asked. "Are you comfortable?"

Hardly! I thought.

"Yes, Master."

"You have been a naughty, naughty girl, haven't you, Slut?"

I agreed.

"And you need to be punished for your sins, don't you?"

I assented again.

"Confess one of your sins to me," he demanded.

The first thing that occurred to me was the bad thing Mamma imagined I had been doing with Timmy O'Shaunessy that last time when I was young. Daddy had never punished me for that because he had left home to play house with Mrs. Dugan.

"I played patty-cake with Timmy O'Shaunessy," I confessed to the captain.

I could not observe what he had in hand, but the stinging sensation I felt landing on my bare exposed ass felt very much like the paddle Daddy used to keep available to "teach me a lesson."

However, the captain had a stronger arm than Daddy. And the blow hurt like Hell.

I could not withhold a whimper. And inadvertently I screamed out "Daddy!"

Captain Master meted out blow after blow.

And after the sixth excruciating painful spank, the pain morphed, as I knew it would.

The fire from my tingling buns settled down into my crotch and virtually set my snatch afire.

A blast of passion erupted within me, sending a flood of my love juices out of my twat.

The flood was clearly visible to my three tormentors.

As I spasmed in an overwhelming orgasm, they laughed aloud.

I dared not say a thing. I was well aware that speaking without being spoken to was forbidden. I was worried that the cry to Daddy that I had emitted might doom me to being cast off from the ship. But, in my erotic delirium I could not be bothered with pursuing that thought.

The blows continued to fall on my blistering bottom.

A hand grabbed my hair and pulled my head up from where it was hanging over the altar's edge.

My eyes were filed with tears. I could not make out who was grabbing my hair.

Whoever it was was aiming an engorged prick at my mouth.

I gasped from my exquisite pain which allowed my open mouth to receive the throbbing hardon. And as I sucked and sucked on that organ a second urgency built up in my gash.

In my excitement I sucked that cock with greater and greater fervor.

And as I came in the throes of the most powerful orgasm I had ever experienced my mouth was filled with the familiar taste of jism which exploded furiously into it.

And, in my overwhelming passion, I passed out.

The agony and joy had been more than I could take.

I did not awaken until the next morning. The room I was in was pitch dark. My body ached all over but the tenderest quarter of all was my tingling ass.

I attempted to sit up and hit my head. The ceiling was only about a yard from the floor.

Ouch!

I reached my arms out to the side and bumped the walls. My room was only about a yard wide.

I had no mattress. I was lying on a cold floor.

Am I in a coffin? Panic!

I had to pee. What to do?

My right foot hit against a cold object. I managed to get the thing up into my hands. It was a crock. A crock? My kind tormentors had left me at least a chamber pot in my cramped quarters.

What sweethearts.

I had no sooner emptied my bladder into the pot than light flooded into my "room."

"Time to get up, Cupcake," the captain's voice boomed into my ears.

I eased off the pot and maneuvered out of my den and out into the corridor that ran the length of the below deck span.

"Reach in and fetch your goddam pot," he ordered. "You want to empty it, don't you?"

"Yes, Master," I answered reflexively.

I blinked at the den that had been provided for my comfort. It was nothing more than a yard-high, two-yard long floor-closet.

So that was going to be my cabin for the length of my sea voyage.

When I retrieved my pottie, I closed the door. My master was standing there, nude and aroused, with a leash in hand. He ogled my naked body and snapped the leash onto my torque ring. As he led me down the corridor by my leash I felt quite subjugated, carrying my pisspot carefully so as not to spill anything as the ship rocked.

Master led me up the steps to the deck and to the railing. I emptied my piss overboard into the Atlantic.

The captain tugged at my leash and led me back below-deck to the galley.

The crew was gathered at a table. There were three of them. All as nude as I had last seen them.

I figured out there could only ever be three of the four sailors present at one time. They rotated the navigation of the steamer among themselves. Someone clearly had to be at the helm at all times.

The three in the galley were Aiden (Master A), Bates (Master Bates) and, of course O'Sullivan (Master Captain) who had just arrived leading Poontang (me) by the leash.

Fu (Master Fu), the cook, had to be at the helm in the top-deck cabin.

Master pointed to a bowl on the floor, attached my leash to an eyebolt on the wall, and took a seat.

I settled down on the floor to see what was in my bowl.

It was my breakfast. Cubes of Spam floating in some canned peas. I took it that Master Fu was scarcely a gourmet chef.

The men were eating a similarly disgusting meal.

Apparently they were the slobs I took them for.

Master Bates ceased eating his slop and began to stroke his handsome dong into a boner.

He got up from the table, still jacking off, took my leash off its hook and led me over to the table where he sat down.

"Suck my dick," he ordered.

"Yes, Master," I responded.

Actually a couple of swallows of jism appealed to me more than the slop in my bowl.

So I contentedly sucked the hunk's cock until I'd swallowed what would have to pass as breakfast.

I was instructed to put my bowl of food in the refrigerator to save it for lunch.

Captain Master looked at his wristwatch.

"Time for Chapel, everyone," he announced.

A happy cheer went up from Bates and Aiden and I was led by my leash to the saintly chapel I had visited the previous day.

CHAPTER THREE

Fun and Games Aboard Ship

I am a fast learner. I had already learned that "chapel" translated into "boys' game room." I could not help but wonder what delights awaited at chapel this morning.

As I was being led to "chapel time," the ship was beginning to rock quite a bit. "Rough seas ahead" I thought to myself. But I suspected that the real rough stuff would take place more in the form of domination by the boys than in the action of the sea.

As Captain Master led me to the door of the chapel, hauling me by my leash, I heard the sounds of drum-beats inside. I knew it had to be two drummers, because where was a steady heavy repetitive beat setting a bass for some very virtuosic rhythms.

Daddy had a pretty good CD collection which we used to listen to together when we were doing our "happy father and daughter" family thing. We both could listen together for hours to the bongo rhythms of Changuito and Almendo. And to Kalani's virtuoso beats on his deep-toned drum.

Daddy and I often had these intimate father-daughter times together after he had "taught me a lesson."

Ever since then I have associated bongo-beat with bottom-beat. I feel both deep within my being.

"Knock off the goddam music, Mates," the captain ordered as we entered the chapel.

"Put your drums aside and bring me those lipsticks from that table on the starboard partition."

The two musical sailors, of course, complied as Captain and I stood waiting.

"We're going to paint some targets on you, Poontang," Captain told me. "We want to pretty up some of the delights we plan to feel, probe, kiss, lick, fuck, bite and nibble. You would like that, wouldn't you?"

"I would adore it, Captain Master," I replied.

I knew that I would probably get punished later for the irony and sarcasm I couldn't keep out of my voice. But then, I knew punishment awaited me no matter what I said.

Captain addressed my lips with his tube of lipstick. I was aware that he was painting enormous clown type lips on my face. He was purposely making my face grotesque. It was humiliating and depressing.

"I know you want me to redden your nose for you, Cunt," he laughed. "Your schnoz is not a target. No way will any of our dongs fit up either of your nostrils. But since you're merely a droll bitch not worth a shit, we'll give you a nose job to go with those clownish cocksucking lips."

He did not expect an answer so I wisely kept my thoughts to myself.

Master A was working on my tits with his lipstick. I could very clearly feel what he was doing.

He began with my aureoles. He ran the stick around and around, in extending circles, to make the haloes appear to cover a good third of each breast. He then pinched, sucked and bit each nipple until it blossomed out to its fullest extension. Then he teased each nub with lipstick until it must have shone. When he stood up before me after finishing his task, his lips were smeared red from sucking all over my lipsticked boobs.

The weirdest sensation of all came from my rear.

Master Bates was back there drawing a large circle around the center of each bun.

Then, strangest of all, he separated my cheeks and applied lipstick to my asshole. It must have made the bud there look the size of a bottle cap.

When he'd finished, he stuck his wet tongue in my ear.

When I got over shuddering from that sensation he told me:

"I've decorated your ass so that it is appealing as Hell. I'm going to lick it, suck it, and probe it with my tongue. And then I might just fuck it before we're through with you today."

I got goosebumps all over. That was the best offer I'd had all day.

Bates and Aiden stood before me as Captain descended onto his knees to do my twat with the God damned lipstick.

First he drew a wide circle around my mound.

"A truly precious target," he commented.

Within that circle he drew a tighter circle around my gash.

"More precious yet," he commented.

As moisture formed where he was decorating me he ran his tongue up and down my slit.

"Mmm-mmm-good," he exclaimed.

The next circle within circles now was inscribed around my clit hood.

He lifted the hood, gave a rough kiss to the gentle nub and was rewarded by another flushing of my nectar onto his lips.

Now each of my swains prepared to take liberties with my decorated parts.

But first they had to march me over to a large mirror hanging from the portside wall so I could see myself.

And what a sight I was. I hadn't had a chance to comb or brush my hair since I'd been taken out of my closet sleeping-den. My clown face was truly bizarre. The ugly clown lips abetted by the red nose was truly disgusting. My tits had been transformed into monstrosities with aureoles and nipples that made me smile despite myself. But I dared not laugh.

My cunt had been made into a series of targets that seemed to say "fuck me". And my ass…! The circles there were simply too much. I *did* chuckle. And got a very smart spanking for it.

The crew had transformed me from a human being into a caricature. I was now no longer even "poontang." I was the legendary "painted woman."

What a humiliation! What a gas!

They hauled me back to the center of the room to engage in their further assaults on me.

One at a time they inserted their fingers into my mouth. I sucked each finger as it slid in and out between my clenched lips as they fingerfucked my yap. Oh, how those lubricated digits shone and gleamed when they emerged covered with my enthusiastic spit.

Captain Master dropped down onto his knees in front of me. One of his spit slicked fingers began to examine the lipstick painted cleft between my thighs. He slipped two fingers inside my kooze and began pumping in a slow seductive rhythm.

I just began giving myself wholeheartedly over to the rhythm when he slipped his fingers out and I felt his lips encircling my lipstick painted mound. The abrupt change caused me to reciprocate involuntarily with increased moisture.

He narrowed his focus to my clit, which was, of course, haloed by its own lipstick. He sucked it in between his teeth and lightly bit down on it.

Yikes! What a sensation.

He withdrew, snaked his tongue out and took a juicy lick around the hard pebble my clit had grown into. Again, he withdrew and tweaked and frantically sucked on that precious love bud of mine.

God! I was frantic. I was ready and desperate to come.

And then…he stood up and looked me in the eye.

"Do you know what that nub on your passion bud is called, whore?"

What the fuck was that all about?

All I wanted was to come. Not answer stupid questions.

"No, Master," I answered. "I do not know."

He slapped me twice across the face. Good hard wallops.

"It's called the *glans clitoridis*, you stupid cow!" he screamed. "As a teacher you should have known that. You will be punished for being such a dumb-ass."

While all that was going on at my twat, I was being simultaneously serviced by the other two sailor boys.

Talk about multiple distraction.

While Captain was down on his knees doing my twat, Aiden was standing behind him paying all kinds of attention to my tits.

He pressed them tightly against each other creating an exquisite pain that made my head swim.

While he pressed the orbs together he nuzzled his face into the resulting cleft, burrowing in with his lathing tongue. With his face buried into the cleavage he kneaded the globes with his large hands, pressing deliberately into the nipples and forcing them to deliciously extend outward.

He then concentrated on one boob at a time.

Biting, at first gently, then ferociously, at each nipple, he engorged each to pebble into hard little points. Once at their extreme extension, he fluttered his tongue over them while rubbing his rough thumbs viciously around the now overly sensitive painted aureoles. He sucked those nipples deep into his ravening mouth and held them in agonizing suspension there.

Combined with what my other two tormenters were doing to me, I was ready to convulse.

But I knew I dared not come yet. The boys needed to keep me in a heightened state of deferred rapture.

With tits and twat engorged by the joint actions of Captain and Aiden, that stud-muffin Bates was busily occupied with my ass.

He had begun by fondling my lipstick encircled cheeks. Then moved around taking love-bites from their outside edges in towards my crack.

Ooo! Goosebumps all over my ass!

With his long-fingered hand he separated my buns, exhibiting the rosy lipsticked bud of my asshole for his full inspection.

I knew it was his pinkie, the little finger of one hand, that drew circles around my sphincters. When the boys had finger-fucked my mouth, Bates had done me with his pinkies as well as his other digits. I'd wondered why at the time. Now I knew he was lubricating them to treat my bum.

Yikes! With one hand spreading my palpitating bunghole, the little finger of the other hand commenced a tentative entry into the hole. Despite my awareness of what Captain and Aiden were doing to me, my shudder at the intrusion up my ass by dream-boy's little finger was the predominant cause of the convulsive shudder that caused my pussy to drench.

I deliberately clenched my ass-ring around that adorable little finger, giving it a welcoming love squeeze.

Bates responded by replacing the pinkie with a thicker lubricated finger. Then another, and another, and, in turn, another. And finally, O Heavens above, his massive thumb.

When his thumb pulled out of my asshole, it snapped shut with a loud pop. The sound was somehow humiliating. But I did not have time to think about that. Because Bates' thickly salivated tongue was now circling the rosebud of my asshole. Ooo! That precious tongue came to a rounded point and…yikes. I was being tongue-fucked up my asshole. In and out, in-out, in out. Slowly at first.

And still, I dared not come.

Then, in concert, all three of my guys got into the same rhythm and produced a symphony of passion within my throbbing body.

I was being worked up to a massive crescendo when…

No, no, no! Don't stop! For God's sake, don't leave my body stranded here!!!

They were not going to allow the ecstasy to peak.

Captain's commanding voice addressed me:

"No, Poontang. Do not dare to come. We know your clit is braced to explode. Your nipples are engorged to the point of paroxysm. And your asshole is yearning for a butt-fuck.

"But all we have been doing is just readying you to be hung on the cross in expiation for being such a shameless whore.

"But before you get the privilege of martyring yourself on the cross, you need to be anointed.

"The sacrificial lamb, no, the sacrificial pig, is what you are, because you're such a swinish slut. So you need to be anointed by the three inquisitors. Lie down there on the floor, face up, spread eagle."

I lay down as directed.

Captain had picked up a bamboo switch and gave me a lashing across my tits.

Ow! That really *smarted. Jeesh!*

"Spread your legs farther apart, Tart! We want a good gander at Poontang's poontang."

The three sports were standing around me, ogling my supine body. Their eyes were staring down. But the eyes of their peters were observing the ceiling. Their hardons, firmly grasped by undulating fists, were definitely stretching mightily heavenwards.

I exerted that last stretch of my thighs to reveal my koozie as blatantly as possible.

"Now," Captain commanded. "Bring both hands down to your mound and stretch your pussy lips wondrously wide for us."

Ah! That feels good. Particularly with those six horny eyes gazing down at my garden of delights.

"Now, you're nothing more than a two-bit whore," the captain sneered. "Like a good cheep whore, I want you to fluff off for us. You know. To use Mister Webster's word for it, masturbate.

"You are already aroused, Broad. But you must not come yet. At that magic moment before the final surge, remove your fingers from your cunt and play with your tits and your asshole. Anything to keep up the suspense but that will withhold final satisfaction as well.

"If you come before I command you to, I have this bamboo switch on the ground next to me that I will retrieve and administer ten hearty lashes right across your nipples and another ten squarely into your snatch. You will find out I am very accurate in my aim. So unless you're looking for more pain than you've ever felt before, DO NOT COME.

"However, we three men standing over you will be jacking off. And we are going to come. We will come all over you. And I want you to bring yourself off the exact moment when we shoot our wads."

With that they set to pumping their cocks with as much enthusiasm as I was applying to my cunt, my clit, my tits and my asshole. We were engaged in a race, but in a race in which we all intended to arrive at the finish line in a dead heat.

My clit was tingling. Ooo!

From the throbbing red crowns of their quivering dicks I knew when the moment was ripe for me to massage my hard clit to orgasm.

Whee!!

We all managed to spasm together.

I flooded the floor with my cunt juices.

They each spurted their jism and managed to aim so that every drop hit my naked body rather than the floor.

God, was I ever a mess.

And Lordie, was I ever relieved, exuberant, and pleased.

Captain commanded me to rub my hands to spread the jism evenly all over my face, tits, belly and kooze.

Then, when I was well anointed, I got to lick the remainder that clung onto my hands off and swallow it.

I guessed that I was now ready to get hung on the cross.

As I was marched up to that simple looking cross I became aware that it was a more complex contraption than met the casual eye.

The vertical beam was fixed to the wall. But I now observed that there was more than one crossbeam. In addition to the obvious horizontal beam there was one not as noticeable at first resting at floor level. Both these crossbars were studded with spaced eyebolts placed at judicious intervals the better to attach hand and ankle cuffs to.

Both crossbars could be extended out into the room away from the vertical bar to a distance of about ten feet.

And, equally cleverly constructed, the crossbars could be raised and lowered.

The upper crossbar was lowered by Master A, who was clearly the resident handyman type. When it was at a height that made it possible for my manacled arms to be easily attached to the bolts, I found that I was actually quite comfortable hanging there.

Oops!

Aiden ratcheted the damned bar up about one foot and, ouch! I found myself dangling rather uncomfortably. My shoulder sockets complained something fierce.

The bottom bar was then raised to a height where I could support myself on it.

Neat! Relief!

Sweet-face, a.k.a. Master Bates, grabbed my ankles, spread my legs as far apart as he could without ripping my body in half, and attached my ankles to the lowbar, destroying the momentary comfort I had enjoyed.

So there I was, hanging spread-eagle on the contraption, rendered more helpless than I had ever found myself in my life.

Bound? Yes. Submissive? Yes. Dominated? Yes. Covered all over with jism? Yes, that too.

What girl wouldn't be delighted with such a turn of fate?

Captain Master strode in front of me, leering evilly and brandishing that bamboo switch he'd used to lash me mercilessly across my hooters just a while ago.

And I knew what was up. Show time, Folks!

He approached me dangling the bamboo switch before my eyes.

And as a preview of things to come he whipped my belly three times with the damned instrument.

Ouch! Jeesh! Screech!

"Now, you filthy cunt," he sneered. "I told you you'd be punished for not knowing the name of the tip of your clit. Do you remember the correct answer now?"

"Yes, Master. It's *glans clitoridis.*"

"That was a good girl," he told me.

He wet a finger and gave a sweet little massage to the member we were discussing.

Ahh!

"Just so you will never forget, there's a stinging reminder," he told me.

One lashing across my clit with that switch had me screaming, sobbing and devastated.

It also caused my pussy to drench.

Next, the captain played the game my daddy, the headmaster and he, himself seemed to relish so much. The inquisitor charged with punishing little girls.

"You were a naughty little girl in your youth, weren't you, Bitch?"

"Yes, Master," I replied.

"For this service," he told me. "You may address me as 'Daddy' if you wish.

"You would like to remember when you were naughty and wanted your father to punish you for it, wouldn't you?"

I felt a buzz in my pussy. That sounded like the best idea I had heard in a while.

"Yes, Daddy," I exulted. "I would like that very much."

"All right, then, Darling," he demanded. "Tell me what naughty thing you are anxious to confess to the three of us."

"Well, Daddy. I let little Timmy O'Shaunessy stick his hard little wee-wee up my bum," I lied.

Actually, as you know, despite the fact that little Timmy and I had never done a single bad thing together, I'd had to confess lots and lots of things we had done to Daddy so he could do the throbbing tent thing in his pants and spank me to his (and my) heart's content.

I could see that my confession had the same effect on the captain that it had had on Daddy. He didn't have any pants on, but he made a tent pole all the same.

"You were a miserable sinning little bitch," he spat out. "The Good Book calls that sodomy and dictates that you must be severely punished. How many swats do you deserve?"

"Three, Daddy?" I ventured looking at the bamboo switch he had in his hand.

Bates strode over to the side table, picked up a very mean, ugly looking cat-o'-nine-tails, brought it to his captain who now had both a whip and his switch in hand.

Oh-oh! Not good! The switch is one thing…but…

"Three, you say, you fucking slut? What do you think of three times three?"

"I think that's nine, Daddy."

"Right you are, you brat. You let Timmy cornhole you, remember. Three times three times three is more like it. What is three times three times three?"

I did not want to say the number. I knew it would be twenty-seven. And I certainly did not want the captain to flog me that many times with that cruel flogger hanging from his right hand. So I did not answer.

He walked up to me and slapped me a good one across my face.

"Do I have to teach you arithmetic, Poontang? Do you know what three times three times three is?"

"Twenty-seven, Master?" I replied hesitatingly.

"Spin the bitch around, Mate," Captain ordered Aiden.

And that mechanical wizard, Master A, flipped a lever that affected my two crossbars and in a mind boggling moment I was swung around facing the wall with the vertical bar on it and my ass now facing the captain, who, I knew, was flicking his flogger in preparation to administer a punishment such as I had never felt before.

He stepped around to where he now faced me in my newly acquired direction.

He set the nasty-looking flogger down on the floor.

Sigh. Relief! That whip is a mean-looking mother.

Captain had the switch in hand now. I knew, first hand, that it inflicted pretty heavy pain. But not like what that damned cat-o'-nine-tails was capable of imposing.

So there I was facing the captain.

I wondered about the location of the other two mates. They had to be somewhere behind me. I could tell what the captain had in mind. But what about Stud-muffin and the handyman?

I felt a pair of hands on my hips. I jumped. Well, it was not actually a jump. I was trussed up too tight for an actual hop. It ended up more like a writhe.

It was enough to cause the three men to laugh aloud.

Personally, I did not find my reaction that amusing.

The hands slipped from my hips down onto my buns. I had no idea who those hands belonged to. So I fantasized them belonging to that yummy Bates.

The hands fondled my cheeks.

Ooo! Sweet.

It made my cunt and my ass-crack clench.

Wait, now. New sensation. The hands kept playing with my butt. But the person standing back there began to breathe on my neck. Then he nibbled at the nape. What a wonderful, exciting feeling.

I couldn't even concentrate on the captain who was flipping that whip of his with one hand while entertaining his Johnson with the other.

Darting out from the love-bites on my neck was a warm, wet tongue.

A shudder of pleasure shot from the nape of my neck right down to that sensitive spot between the ass and the pussy called the perineum.

The captain had his Latin words to teach me. I probably could have taught him that one. But I never found the occasion

We teacher types know lots of things by their Latin names.

You may not know that delightful spot down there by its name. But I'll bet anything you've rested a finger there from time to time when you've been masturbating, haven't you?

That wet tongue began to make a descent. As the warm, slick tongue rode down my spine the hands left my buns and held tightly onto my hips.

As he sank down onto his knees the busy fellow's tongue made its descent down along with him. And the tongue trail was accompanied by periodic nibbles and slurpy kisses on my delighted skin.

I could take this all day long.

I had to suppress the giggles that formed in my mouth.

As his tongue approached my ass-crack, I had to clench and unclench that cleft spasmodically.

You would have thought I was doing some kind of hootchy-kootchy dance from the wiggly motions allowed me by my bondage.

Those loving hands slipped back down off my hips onto my buns. Oh, the sensual massage those hands played over those mounds.

Whoa! Not only massages but accompanying love nips appeared here, there and everywhere over my ass.

I got goosebumps on my goosebumps.

The hands gave up their delightful wandering over the cheeks and started delving into my ass-crack and separating the cheeks.

I knew the dude, whoever it was, now had a first-class focus on my asshole.

Hello? Want me to wink at you?

I clenched and unclenched the sphincters of that puckered-up rosy orifice. If there ever was an invitation being made, I was making it, Brother.

I could not help but wonder what would follow. Perhaps a probing finger? If so, I hoped it would be his pinkie.

Whoa! It was a pinkie, all right. But hardly what I expected.

A slick wet tongue was playfully circling the crinkly halo surrounding the hole.

Ooo! Makes my nipples and my clit pebble out!

My groin got more than damp. Drenched would be a more apt description.

I wondered what delicious thing would happen next.

Wham!

The sailor-boy ran his stiff tongue right into my asshole. And as that lubricious entry occurred the captain approached in front of me and whipped my tits with his goddam whisk.

Ooh! Ouch! Whee! Jeesh!

Pleasure and pain flooded over my entire body at the same time.

I was getting a tittie-whip and a tongue-cornhole at the same time. In perfect sync.

Every time that erotic tongue probed in I got a very smart whisk across my engorged nipples. Could I stand it?

In and out. Slash...slash...Jesus, that smarts!...ooh!

It was excruciatingly painful. It was excitingly pleasurable.

Tiny shocks reverberated throughout my body.

I shrieked. I moaned. I sighed. I cried.

I grew more and more impassioned.

The pain from the whisk accompanied by the tongue sodomizing my ass meshed into an ache of arousal that caused me to shudder with ecstasy.

On the tenth lashing of my boobs, accompanied by the tenth thrust of that glorious tongue up my asshole, I came with a squeal of passion erupting from the tingles of my twat to the hair-roots of my scalp.

The tongue abruptly withdrew from my asshole.

The captain tossed his bamboo switch off to the side of the room.

"All right, Poontang," he told me. "That's ten of the twenty-seven lashes you asked for. How many more does that leave for this session?"

I was so shaken by the experience I'd just undergone I could not summon a single word in response.

He stepped up to me with palm extended.

Jesus, the last thing I needed at the moment was one of his vicious smacks across my kisser.

Ouch!

But I got it anyway.

"Seventeen," I managed to say through my deluge of tears.

That cursed switch was no longer in his other hand. Which, I supposed, should have been a relief. Except that in its place he was gripping that frightening cat-o'-nine-tails. The exchange of whips did not seem to bode well for my future comfort.

My captain smirked and stepped around behind as Bates took his place in front of me.

Did that mean that it was this hunk, after all, who had been regaling me with the scrumptious tongue-fucking up my asshole while I was getting the tittie-whipping? The thought dampened my groin anew.

All I could concentrate on was that handsome boner pointing up at me from beneath Bates' ripped abs.

I wanted to get fucked. I needed to get fucked. I'd go crazy if I didn't get fucked.

And there was the prick primed and ready to do the job.

I began to drool.

Master Bates approached me and pressed that gorgeous hunk of quivering meat against my beaver.

He leaned the upper part of his body back so he could tweak my nipples. Those babies were sore as hell from being roundly switched by Master Captain. Ten times, for cripe's sake.

But, God, was that dudely Bates ever good at nipple tweaking.

He twisted, he kneaded, he rubbed, he pulled, he yanked, he pinched. It hurt like Hell. It hurt so *good!*

He worked those pebbled nubs until they were extended beyond belief.

In the meantime, I tried to squirm up to where I could fit his pulsating dong into my hole.

But, no way. My tight bondage did not allow even a quarter-inch of squiggle.

But, God damn it. I needed to come. I had to have that peter up into my yearning heaven.

Sorry! No can do.!

Shit! The bastard pulled his dick away from my bush. It had been so excruciatingly cozy there.

Come back, Big Boy!

But what's he doing now?

His face zoomed in on my hooters.

Jesus! He's going to suck my tits. Oh, great. My nipples were literally jumping with joy in expectation of the coming treat.

His manly lips encircled one of my pebbled nipples.

Ahh! The sweet suckling sent shiver after shiver throughout my body.

And his hand was strumming the other nipple.

Ouch! He took a bite. Sucking's one thing. Biting's another.

Well, not bites really. Nibbles. Even on a nipple that's been whisked, tender, sore, needy. It's a love-pain.

My nipples, indeed the entire orbs, were extremely sensitive and painful from the lashing they had received from the switch. But the mixture of pleasure and pain was yielding me ecstasy.

Zing! Ouch! Goddam!

The first flash of the nine-tailed cat landed squarely across my back.

The first of seventeen?

I shrieked with pain. My eyes filled with tears. My cunt filled with elixir.

With the strike of the knotted leather strands on my back Bates shifted the breast he was entertaining.

Zing!

That one raised welts on my lower thigh. Stings like Hell.

Pow!

Bates shifted tits. The cat sliced across my shoulders.

"I've marked the 'strike zone' for you, Poontang,," Captain shouted at me. "Thighs to shoulders. I'm accurate with my cat, Darling. Your pretty neck and lovely calves won't feel the bite at all."

Well, I guessed that that was about as much good news as I was likely to get for a while.

His blows did stay within the strike zone. And more slashed on my ass than anywhere else.

The pleasure-pain was as strong at my tits as what I was experiencing from my lashing.

I shrieked, I moaned, I bellowed, I cried and I spasmed at each and every blow of the cat.

"Please feel free to scream," Captain laughed. "It's music to my ears."

Bates pulled his mouth from my boobs long enough to say, "Mine, too."

Then he applied his lips and tongue to the boob of the moment with renewed vigor.

The bastard! The sweetheart!

As he continued sucking, Bates had slipped his hand down to pet my bush.

Ahh!

I'd lost count of the lashings on my back. The rapture had overcome me as that masculine hand slipped down from my beaver to my cunt.

As he palmed my mound I screamed. I was sure that the squeal was indistinguishable from my cries of pain. But it was an expression of pure pleasure that erupted from my throat.

My koozie was drenching. I knew I was filling Bates' loving, probing hand with bountiful flows of my cream.

A finger inserted itself into my hole.

I felt as if my loins were melting and burning.

My twat was creaming ever more copiously with the moisture running over Bates' hand and down my legs.

A voice behind me was counting. With each application of the lash a number was being shouted out.

An awareness of the numbers merged with the feelings I was experiencing. Excruciating pain. Poignant pleasure.

The voice. It wasn't the captain's. It was the engineer's. Aiden was chanting the numbers. What were they?

"Twelve...thirteen...fourteen..."

Bates was filling his hands with my silky nectar. He began to smear my juices all over my clit.

Did I want the flogging to stop at this point?

If it did, would the erotic exhilaration I was feeling dissipate with it?

Bates fell to his knees. He was licking his tongue all over and around the pulsating nub of my clitoris.

I heard the captain's loud, boisterous, vulgar laugh and shout.

"Look at the goddam slut. She's like a two-bit whore. She loves to be whipped while she's being pussy-licked."

Aiden continued his count.

"Fifteen...sixteen...seventeen!"

I whimpered. It was over.

What was I moaning about? Because I desperately needed to come? Or because the torture was over?

Frankly, I did not know. I still don't.

Bates had risen from his knees.

He was staring at me with a silly grin on his handsome face.

There was fire at my ass.

Suddenly, a new sensation.

Someone was running his tongue over the welts on my ass.

Painful. Soothing. Lovely.

The stinging pain became pleasure as that person behind me changed from licking to running his teeth over the fiery welts.

When the lips, tongue and teeth had completed their tour of my ass, Aiden stepped in front of me.

He began to manipulate the crossbars that held me in my suspended bondage and rotated my ravaged body to face back into the room. Then he pushed the crossbars back to where they met the vertical bar so that the original cross was composed again.

I was aware that all three men were engaged in the process of freeing me from my bondage and were lowering the body they had been torturing and pleasing from the cross.

I passed out, exhausted and exhilarated as never before.

In my unconscious state I was transported back to my dark closet den to sleep.

Blessed, blessed sleep.

When I finally awoke I was confused and disoriented. It was dark. So dark. Was it daylight or dark outside? Morning, noon or night?

And I hurt. Oh, how I hurt. My bosom, particularly my nipples. I felt them and cringed.

I was lying on my back on a hard surface. It felt like wood. And every place where the skin of my back made contact with that wooden surface was blazing with pain.

And in the midst of the dark, the pain and the horror, my fingers took refuge at my cunt. I was barely awake, yet I had two fingers working up and down my love channel while three fingers of the other hand were strumming sweet music on my clit.

Pressure was mounting within my whole body. Come. I had to come.

Despite my pain and confusion there was only one thing that mattered to me. I had to get myself off.

Mounting intensity. Madder and madder fluffing off! Can't hold back another second!! Yikes!!!

My scream resounded within the restricted space I found myself in.

Just as I let out that joyful blast of exaltation the door to my closet den swung open letting in a glaring burst of light that blinded me.

"Well, well," Captain Master's voice greeted me. "I see we're enjoying ourselves this morning. Nothing like a good orgasm to get ourselves up and going, is there?"

He reached in, pulled me roughly out of my space while I was still shivering and pulsating from my climax.

He fastened my leash to my torque.

Oh, I suddenly knew where I was again. And recollections of my tortures sometime in the recent past were revived by the painful welts that marked my abused body.

"You can stand up, Wench," he assured me. "I'm way too compassionate a fellow to make you crawl to the galley on all fours."

Hah! What a line of bullshit. Imagine the balls of the man to get off a line like that after he'd flayed me so mercilessly…when? Yesterday?

I heard the sound of the bongo drums filling the passageway as I crawled towards the galley.

The captain led me by my leash into the galley. He pointed to my spot on the floor where my dish had some kind of slop waiting for me that was about as appealing as the other food Fu prepared for us.

The crew, minus Fu, was seated at the table looking mournfully at their breakfast bowls.

Those lads needed a new cook as badly as I did.

Bates and Aiden were playing a pretty good duet on their bongos rather than spooning into their slop.

That drum music haunts me to this day whenever I recall my experiences on the *Submissive Miss.*

"I've got to pee," I said.

Captain unhooked my leash.

"The pot's in that cabinet," he told me while pointing in a direction.

"Go get it and take it to your corner."

I found the pot and did as he said.

"Don't I get any privacy?" I asked.

The lugubrious looks on the lads' faces brightened and they all broke out into joyful laughter.

That was my answer.

So I squatted over the damned pottie and let go.

With the way the boat was still rocking and bouncing over the waves, it was no mean trick to hit the pot.

There was a paper napkin next to my food bowl. The "gentlemen" stared at my crotch as I wiped myself off.

Bastards!

After breakfast, Captain re-attached my leash.

I picked up my pottie and was led out to empty the contents into the foamy brine.

I was led back to the galley to store the mug into its cupboard.

Everyone had left the galley and I had a feeling it was party time and that I was the guest of honor. Or, perhaps, more pithily stated, the entertainment.

I was led back to the stern. "The poop deck" I called it.

The crew was assembled there with the exception of Aiden. He clearly had relieved Fu at the helm.

"Look at the present we got for you, Poontang," the captain exclaimed happily.

"Where, Master?" I wondered, uncomfortable about what I might find.

"In your favorite dingy, Sweetheart," Captain informed me.

I looked into "my" dinghy.

And what to my wondering eyes did appear?

A rubber dildo had been affixed to the seat. It was pointing proudly at the cloudless blue sky above.

It glistened. It had been well lubricated.

How thoughtful.

"It's flexible," Captain informed me. "When you sit down in your little boat, you'll find that you can impale yourself on it up the cunt or up the ass. Your choice. Get in!"

So get in I did. And I fit that eight inch long dong right up my twat.

OOO! Not so bad.

It would be better if there weren't those horny guys gawking at me as I settled into my cozy impalement. But what choice did I have?

"This is the latest treat we have for you, Love," Captain told me in false cooing terms.

"We're giving you an hour or so to ride the waves every day until we reach America. And lucky you. The waves are particularly choppy today. You'll get a jolly sea-fuck. We're sure you'll love it. You're such a slut."

So I was hoisted up in my boat and lowered into the ocean below, the prow of my dinghy, *Dependence*, connected by the sturdy rope to the poop deck of the good ship *Submissive Miss*.

I was towed along on a bumpy ride over the turbulent waves with a dildo up my cunt, enjoying being fucked by King Neptune himself.

A girl could get used to this.

CHAPTER FOUR

Sweet Land of Liberty

The tramp steamer chugged its way across the Atlantic for sixteen days. One day melted into another for me. I grew accustomed to submitting to any humiliation or punishment any member of the crew chose to lavish on me. I dutifully thanked each one for abusing me. And I was inwardly delighted to learn the joy of bondage, discipline and submission.

As the ship approached the New World I was totally hooked on being dominated.

When the Statue of Liberty hove into view I was riding the bouncing waves in *Dependence* with my dildo giving me what I knew Americans call a cornholing.

America was welcoming me with a glorious orgasm.

I was back on board the *Submissive Miss* when we pulled up to the wharves.

Captain O'Sullivan called me to his cabin while the crew was engaged in securing the boat to the dock.

"Well, Colleen," he addressed me. "Here we are. The end of the voyage."

Colleen! Not Poontang?

"I want you to know the crew and I have enjoyed having you as a passenger."

"Thank you, Master," I replied.

"Tut, tut, Colleen," the captain said. "The terms of your submission are over. A mere 'Captain,' or 'Captain O'Sullivan' will suffice."

Whew!

"Now that you are in America," he continued. "Mister McCarthy's concern for your welfare continues."

He handed me an envelope.

"In this envelope, you will find two hundred dollars. The school master did not want you to be penniless in your new homeland.

"In addition to the money, you will find a name and a telephone number. Your former employer, in his magnanimity, has arranged a job interview for you. The employment is not assured, but he believes you have the necessary qualifications for the position. He even was so kind as to provide you with training for it."

Training? What training? What job?

"The crew and I have exerted every effort to teach you some of the skills you will find useful should you be hired by the people who will interview you."

I knew that Headmaster McCarthy had not provided the measly two hundred dollars and the opportunity to interview for a job in America because of any kind of compassion for me. He was concerned that I would arrive in this new land, be picked up by immigration and be shipped back to Ireland and become an embarrassment to him and to the O'Doul family.

Well, I determined I would make a go of it here in America. And if I ever returned to Ireland, it would be as a rich bitch, not a deportee.

Captain O'Sullivan apparently was no novice at smuggling immigrants into the United States past customs and immigration officials. A small skiff pulled up next to the *Submissive Miss*, I was hustled aboard. And before I knew it I was debarking at a fancy yacht club.

A couple of rich looking lads met me there, took me to a taxi, and before I knew it I was in Times Square.

I got out of the taxi, an Irish lass with no passport, no work permit, a couple of hundred dollars in my purse, a suitcase in hand, a telephone number with a lead to a job interview and a resolve to "make it" in this sweet land of liberty.

Times Square was very exciting. I'd seen it many times before in the movies and on the telly. But they don't do the place justice. I hadn't been to any really large city before. Not even Dublin. So I was unprepared for the exciting pulse of a real metropolis.

I loved it.

The only thing I did not love was the weather.

The New York heat was sweltering. It was hot, humid and oppressive.

But I was not going to let the weather get me down. If the millions of people in this city could deal with it, I knew I could.

But the climate was certainly nothing at all like what I was used to back home. County Cork is not particularly known for its oppressive heat.

I spied a chemist's shop. What the Americans call a drug store.

I marched right up to a clerk in there and told her I wanted to make a telephone call.

She smiled real pretty and said, "You're Irish, aren't you?"

I was so surprised.

"How do you know, Miss?" I asked.

"Your accent," she laughed.

I thought that was right funny myself. She was the one with the accent.

But everyone around me had an accent. An American accent. I told her that and we had ourselves a good laugh together.

She gave me change for one of the American bills I had and told me where there was a pay phone.

I found it easy enough where she said it would be and pushed the buttons with the numbers on them.

A strong male voice answered.

"Hello."

"Hello," I said. "I'd like to speak to Mister Zachary Lund."

"I am Zachary Lund," was his answer. "And I'll just bet you're Colleen O'Merry."

You could have knocked me over with a feather. I was at a loss for words

"You see," the voice explained. "I was informed that you had landed here in New York a short time ago. And with your accent..."

Accent again. I'd have to get used to the fact that I was the one with the accent here.

McCarthy had been quite thorough. In the short time I'd been in this foreign country someone had kept tabs on me some way.

Well, don't go dumb on the man. Speak up. I told myself.

"I...I'd like to set up an appointment...that is, I was told I could interview for..." I stammered.

"Certainly, Miss O'Merry. You arrived in America recommended. Mister Alex Allen is in town at the moment. He's the head counselor at Camp Robinson Crusoe. It so happens that he is at the Cronyn Hotel at the moment and could meet you at his room there in about an hour. Would that be convenient?"

Jesus! Things were moving right along, weren't they?

"Where is the hotel exactly?" I asked.

"You're calling from Times Square, aren't you?" he asked.

How did he know that? Oh! The lads who'd put me in the taxi cab must be the ones who'd let him know I had arrived and where I had headed.

"Yes, Sir. I'm in a chemist's...drug store here."

"Fine. Get yourself to the corner of Forty-second Street and Tenth Avenue. From that spot you will be able to see the hotel. Mister Allen will be in Room Seven-thirty. He will expect you at one o'clock sharp. He will be accompanied by Jenna Crawly, our crafts counselor.

"Remember one o'clock sharp. Alex is a stickler for promptness so don't be early or late.

"One o'clock. Do you understand?"

"Yes, Sir," I replied.

Click.

He'd hung up without so much as a "good-bye" or a "go to Hell."

Hmm. Americans.

I hustled back to the nice clerk and asked her how I could get to Forty-second Street and Tenth Avenue.

I told her I had enough money to take a cab if it was very far away. I didn't want to try to get on the subway with my suitcase and all. I'd learned from the movies that that could be quite an undertaking.

The nice girl laughed and told me the corner I was looking for was within easy walking distance and which way to head.

So I picked up my suitcase, got myself back into that busy swarm of people on Times Square and set out on my way.

I got to the corner I was headed for in less than fifteen minutes and spotted the Cronyn Hotel.

It was just about noon by then and I'd been warned not to get to my appointment early or late.

There was a coffee shop near by and I'd worked up a bit of hunger so I went in and had myself a ham sandwich and a couple of cups of coffee. And by the time I'd been served and had eaten my sandwich and had my second cup of coffee I knew I could get to my appointment right on the dot of one at Room Seven-thirty at the hotel right down the block.

My short walk from the coffee house to the hotel, carrying my suitcase, had me sweating like Paddy's pig. New York would take some getting used to.

Sure enough, though. At the prick of one I knocked on the hotel door of Room Seven-thirty. I hoped the room would be air conditioned so I could cool off a bit.

The door opened and my heart skipped a beat.

A suntanned, broad-shouldered, blonde, square-jawed blue-eyed gorgeous hunk of masculinity flashed his gleaming white teeth at me and extended his hand.

"Hello, there," he smiled. "You must be Colleen O'Merry."

I slid my sweaty palm into his massive grip.

"And I am Alex Allen," he continued.

"How do you do, Mister Allen," I blurted.

"I prefer to go by first names," the gorgeous bloke said. "It's a California thing. May I call you Colleen?"

I assured Mister Good-looking that I would be comfortable with an Alex-Colleen relationship.

As I entered the hotel room I could see that the bed, dresser and desk had been pushed aside to provide the atmosphere of an interview room. There were three utilitarian chairs arranged in a conversation circle in the middle of the room.

Getting up from one of the chairs was a stunning looking olive-skinned girl about my age. She had violet colored eyes, long jet-black hair and high cheekbones. She was skimpily but stylishly dressed. I guessed that her attire was a "California thing" too.

The short-skirted outfit with the low-cut blouse that I'd brought with me from Ireland felt appropriate.

"This is Jenna Crowley," Alex told me. "She is a counselor at Camp Robinson Crusoe. She will sit in on our interview."

The lass shook my hand.

As she shook it she looked me up and down appreciatively.

When I turned back to Alex, he was giving me the once-over as well. Or, to be more precise, the twice- or thrice-over.

"Won't you be seated, Colleen," he invited as he sat his trim ass down on one of the chairs.

When we were settled down he asked:

"Are you aware of the nature of the position we have open?"

I told him that I had no idea of what the job was, the nature of the business, or even its location.

He did not appear surprised and launched into a description that made things clear to me for the first time.

"We run a summer camp on Catalina Island," he began.

When he saw from my expression that I did not have an inkling about where such an island existed he explained Catalina to me and what the enterprise was there that he was involved with.

As you no doubt know, dear reader, Catalina is an island in the Pacific Ocean a few miles off the coast of Southern California. It is a vacation spot with only one city on it, a town actually, called Avalon.

There are summer camps located at the various bays and inlets around the isle. And Camp Robinson Crusoe was, and still is, one such camp located on Defoe Bay.

During the summer, children, mainly from Southern California, arrive for periods of two to six weeks.

The activities at Camp Robinson Crusoe are swimming, water sports, boating, crafts, hiking, horseback riding, campfires, and nearly every other kind of summer camp program you can think of.

"The position we are interviewing for is swimming instructor and water sports coach," Alex told me.

"We were sent a file from a school in Ballycormac, in Ireland, recommending you to us, in which there is a glowing report about the position you held there as instructor and coach."

That old devil McCarthy! What a wily bastard!

"Mister McCarthy wrote that you were heading to America in search of employment. Is that correct?"

I answered him that it was.

The windows in the room were closed. And there was no air conditioning. I was uncomfortable with the humidity and the heat. But I was determined not to pay attention to such trifles. I needed to concentrate on making a good impression so I could get the job.

"Now, you understand," Alex continued, "that we are seeking to employ a person who is content with a summer job. In September we close the camp. But our director, Zachary Lund, has many contacts in the Los Angeles area. If he is impressed by you, there's a better than even chance he will help you find a position in the fall. Would you be interested in a job that only extends through the summer?"

I assured him I was.

"The camp is rather isolated. There are no roads that connect it with the city of Avalon. We have boats that go up to Avalon from time to time. But most of the time you would be pretty much stuck at Defoe Bay. If you were given the position, would you be uncomfortable with the potential isolation?"

"Not at all, Alex," I assured him. "I know I would not be concerned in the least about that."

"There is a legal matter that we will have to discuss," he went on.

Oh-oh! Legal. Like immigration status? I began to perspire more freely.

"Tell me about your passport status and your green card."

"Green card?" I asked.

"Yes. The paper from the United States government granting you permission to seek employment here."

Alex's eyes, and Jenna's, too, seemed to bore into me.

I flushed with despair. I was in a foreign country without a passport or a... "green card."

The couple watching me could tell from the way I was reddening what my status was. Illegal immigrant.

All I could say was "I'm sorry to have bothered you."

I started to get up.

Alex stood up at the same time and bade me sit down again.

"It's not the end of the world, Colleen," he assured me. "From the material your Headmaster McCarthy forwarded to us, we deduced you might arrive at this interview devoid of papers.

"It's all right. If you have the qualifications for the job, you will be safe on Catalina Island. No immigration officers would ever come to Defoe Bay looking for wetbacks."

He saw the confusion in my eyes.

"Wetbacks. That's American slang for illegal immigrants."

I'm sure I looked as relieved as I felt.

"By September, if you are compliant with our needs, Zack has contacts in L.A. who can create a passport for you that is even more realistic than a legal one. And they can forge a green card as well. Not to worry."

"Compliant?" Strange word. "L.A.?" I knew that was what Americans called Los Angeles.

My spirits picked up again.

Why don't they open the windows? We're all sweating like we were in a Turkish bath in here.

Alex proceeded to tell me that he and the director felt sure that my qualifications as a teacher and coach were outstanding. Mister McCarthy's recommendations were glowing.

Then he changed subjects quite abruptly.

"Do you *really* want the position I have described to you, Colleen?"

I gave him my most sincere "Yes."

"I would think so," he declared.

"After all. You are in the United States illegally with no papers and a very limited chance of being hired for even a menial job.

"And we can offer you a job for which you qualify and in which you would undoubtedly find pleasure.

"But there is an element to a staff position at Camp Crusoe I have not yet mentioned. Allow me to explain it to you.

"All of our employees are held to a very rigid level of discipline. Everyone who works at the camp must obey every demand or request of the director and me without question.

"That is for the sake of the safety of the campers and for the public image of our enterprise.

"Are you aware of the meaning and connotations of the word 'discipline'?"

My, but it was getting hotter in that stuffy room.

"Alex," I told him. "I believe I understand the meaning of the word quite well.

"When I was young my father taught me discipline and submissiveness. He firmly believed that sparing the rod would spoil the child. And I assure you, I was not spoiled.

"At Ballycormac, Headmaster McCarthy punished me for an infraction by slapping me around, forcing me to commit fellatio on him, and submitting to bondage, humiliation and flogging.

"I willingly submitted myself to that punishment, which I richly deserved.

"I survived the chastisement, thanking him, as I thank my father for giving me the chance to expiate for my shortcomings.

"On the ship that brought me to these shores, I suffered more daily bondage, beatings and humiliation than I had ever encountered from my father or the headmaster.

"If discipline and submission are qualities you and the director are looking for in an employee, I am sure you will find me very qualified."

I was desperate to get the job at the camp. I hoped I had laid it on thick enough.

Alex smiled at Jenna. It was clearly a signal. I felt that the smile signified that I had passed some kind of preliminary screening.

I was pretty sure that the next phase of the screening that I was undergoing had commenced when Alex said, "It is beastly hot in here," as he stood up and removed his coat.

The hot stuffiness of the room made sense to me at once. If I really wanted the job, I would need to demonstrate submissiveness. And, I would need to respond to the master's subtle hints.

I'd been initiated enough into the mysteries of dominance, submission and bondage to be able to pick up thinly disguised invitations.

This hunk's dominant nature was revealing itself in spades.

I looked over at Jenna. She was already stripped down so far all she had to take off was a top.

She removed it, leaving her clad above the waist in only her brassiere.

After removing his jacket, Alex was in his shirtsleeves. His damp, sweat-soaked shirt clung to him, revealing a very well-muscled torso.

Why not? A head counselor at an island summer camp would be an athlete after all. Wouldn't he?

Of course.

Without comment, I stood up and removed my jacket, feeling somewhat overdressed now for the occasion.

My bosom was enhanced with the removal of the garment. I arched my back, though, to emphasize my charms.

Could I help it if my nipples got hard just ogling the guy's muscles outlined against his shirt?

His eyes seemed to dive right down into my cleavage. And I knew he was aware of my pebbled nipples pressing against my damp blouse.

Is that a throbbing I discern at his fly? Easy girl. You don't want to dampen your panties even more in front of your interviewer, now. Or do you?

I could see that Alex was aware of my fascinated glance at his tented crotch.

Really girl. Look at his face, not his groin.

Alex told Jenna to come over to where I was standing to help me off with my blouse.

I did not object or resist.

"Now, Colleen," my interviewer said. "I want you to help Jenna take off her brassiere."

Well, virtually speaking, the heat was really on now.

Jenna turned her back to me.

I unclasped her brassiere and removed it, placing it on the chair behind me.

Her breasts were quite perky and lovely.

Alex, still standing, removed his shirt.

His beautifully sculpted torso made me dampen my panties something fierce.

I could not help it.

But I suspected that the obvious dampness was probably adding points to my candidacy for the job.

"Now, Jenna," he said. "Would you be so kind as to help Colleen off with her brassiere? It's way too warm in here for her to be over-burdened with so much clothing."

Jenna slinked over to me, removed my brassiere and ran her fingers from the nape of my neck to the crack in my ass.

The shudder I experienced was sexually exciting. It made my ass and my pussy clench in unison.

Then, just as my shiver subsided, she reached around me and cupped my boobs in her hand as she pressed her body against me.

I felt my innards seem to drain right down and out my snatch.

Alex asked me, archly, "How badly do you really want the job we're discussing, Colleen?"

"Very much, indeed, Alex," I assured him.

"Enough to demonstrate to me that you can submissively follow instructions?"

"Try me," I boldly proclaimed.

In a masterly, demanding tone he commanded, "Turn around and kiss Jenna. On the mouth!"

I slowly and suggestively turned around, looked into Jenna's eyes, and put my lips to hers.

Her tongue made entrance into my mouth, found my tongue and ran over it with a luxurious sliding motion.

Then she inhaled my tongue like a vacuum.

I had never before kissed or been kissed by another female.

I was surprised at the extent to which it turned me on.

My panties were drenched.

I engaged in a bit of sexy tongue play with her and purposely rubbed my titties against hers.

I could feel her erotic response to my gesture.

Alex's command followed.

"Break up the clinch, girls!"

We responded without the slightest lingering.

"Colleen," he continued. "I want you to suck Jenna's tits."

Her nipples were tastily extended. I put my one hand around and across her back, cupped her left boob, and burrowed into the inviting nubbed breast with tongue and lips.

It got me as hot as when I had previously sucked cock.

What a revelation!

"Break it off, Ladies," Alex demanded all too soon.

"Now let me see you submit to Jenna sucking your tits," was his next order.

Let me tell you. That girl could suck a tit with cunt-heating sophistication.

Just when I thought I was going to have to bring myself off or go nuts, the heart-breaking next order was given.

"Back to your chairs, Girls!"

Oh, damn! And we were having so much fun.

I sat in my chair primly, like an obedient schoolgirl. I awaited his next command.

He's going to tell me to get naked, I guessed.

"Take off the rest of your clothes, Colleen. Including your shoes and stockings."

See? I was right! I just know what these dominant males think like.

I stood up, complied calmly, and sat back down.

There was no question that Alex approved of everything that I had revealed so far for his devouring eyes.

Alex had remained standing for the entire time Jenna and I had been responding to his demands.

The boner pressing against his trousers promised a better than adequate treat waiting for me beating time in there.

"The heat in this room is getting to me, Colleen," Alex complained. "It has made my balls all sweaty. Tell me you would just love to lick the sweat off my balls…and, when you do so, I would like you to address me as 'My Master.'"

Quick as a wink I uttered the phrase he was waiting for.

"O my master. Please allow me to lick the sweat off your hot balls."

I could see that he was pleased with my nifty response.

Why wouldn't he be? It was what he wanted. And the idea had a certain whimsical attraction for me, too.

"Down on your hands and knees and crawl over here, Colleen. May I call you Colleen?"

"I would be most pleased if you were to call me Kate, My Master," I told him.

I went down onto the floor and crawled over to Master Gorgeous Muscles.

"Without getting up, take my shoes, sox, belt, pants and shorts off me," he ordered.

Now there was a treat. I could hardly wait to get an eyeful of the equipment beckoning me behind all that clothing. Including the sweaty balls. Let me at it.

As I removed the articles, he set them neatly aside. He took special care with the alligator belt he had been wearing. I suspected, knowing much now about his nature, that I would become well acquainted with that belt before the interview was over.

Before very long, I had him unclothed.

With his pants off, I got a joyful eyeful of his awesome six-pack, his bright blond bush, and his lovely, mouth-watering prick.

And hanging beneath that solid hardon were the balls which were, as advertised, glistening with sweat.

The master accommodated me by sitting down on the edge of his chair.

His prick pointed up. His wet hairy balls hung down.

He fisted his boner and pumped it up to a glorious fullness as I crawled up to him and began breathing in that musky male scent that always lingers so appetizingly at men's groins.

Now, to engage in getting that scent to coat my taste buds.

I slurped my contented tongue around each of the dangling orbs. I went up the center seam of the scrotum on the back side up to tickle the perineum behind. Then I followed that seam around to the base of his dick.

The wiry hairs tickled my lips.

"Swallow my balls. Now!" my new master ordered.

I opened wide my mouth and took those masterful hot nuts inside. My nose was pressing the base of his staff.

Ah, the musky male perfume. I love it!

My mouth swished the balls around as my tongue played with the contours.

Wicked thought. I was the submissive one. But did it occur to the chap that he was the vulnerable one? There was not a thing he could do about it were I to take it into my head to bite his testicles right off at that moment!

The naughty thought made me laugh.

The stifled laugh, I know, sounded to him like a moan of delight.

"Jenna!" he ordered. "Get your ass over here. I'm going to come and I need your fucking mouth as a receptacle!"

So there I was on my knees with his balls in my playful mouth at one end and Jenna bent over him with the other end of his equipment in her mouth.

I felt his scrotum contract tightly, the balls draw up into the shaft and a shudder coursing from those glands in my mouth, up through his pulsing pecker and thence throughout the rest of his body as Jenna drank in his seed.

It was quite an experience for the three of us.

All of us were both excited and exhilarated by the tripartite experience.

What more could the dreamboat master want or expect?

Well…quite a bit more, as it turned out.

Languidly sprawled out in his chair, he looked down at the girl who had just finished gargling his balls – me.

"Colleen!" he announced. "Poor Jenna's got herself all hot and bothered from the excitement of sucking my dick and swallowing my jism. We can't let her suffer, can we?"

"No, we can't, Master," I agreed.

"Jenna!" he called. "Spread your lovely body out on the floor there, with your feet pulled up by your tush and your knees spread apart as far as you can get them."

Jenna gleefully assumed the pose. Her twat was gloriously exposed to Alex's appreciative view (and mine as well).

"Take your hands and spread your pussy-lips nice and wide now for us, Jenna! Ah, yes. What a lovely smile. Now, with your left thumb, lift up your clit hood.

"Sweet. Isn't that cute, Colleen?"

"Cutest thing I've ever seen, Master," I readily agreed. "Now, Colleen," Alex advised me. "You are going to go down on Jenna and bring her off using only your mouth and tongue. You would like to do that for Jenna, wouldn't you?"

"Nothing would please me more, Master," I told him.

As you know, I had no former experience with what we Irish call "the love that dares not speak its name." But the prospect of nuzzling down into that appealing quim made my own sex quiver with anxious delight.

I started to crawl towards Jenna to suck and lick that desirable cunt when Alex's stern voice stopped me cold.

"It would please me to have your muff-dive accompanied by music, Colleen," he said. "You may stand up, temporarily, and sashay over to the desk by the window. On the desk you will find a lovely pair of nipple clips. They're joined together by a chain. And on that chain are affixed a set of twelve bells that tinkle charmingly when jingled. Bring the article over here to me."

I got up and walked over to the desk. And when I saw the two clips with their wicked alligator teeth, my mood shifted abruptly from delighted to appalled.

Those suckers would hurt like Hell if Alex was going to clip them onto my nipples.

Oh, well. In for a penny, in for a pound.

I brought the damned clips to my sadistic master and handed them to him.

"Kneel down in front of me, Colleen," he ordered.

I did so, of course.

"Arch your back so your hooters aim right at me now," he ordered.

Hooters! I'm learning American. First Poontang. Then muff-dive. Now Hooters.

Alex roughly grabbed one of my nipples in each hand. They were already extended from the erotic tone that prevailed, but he tugged at them, twisted them, pinched them and bent down and sucked them fiercely, ending his stimulation with a painful bite.

I could not suppress a scream and a sob as those gleaming teeth of his bit down into my sensitive nubs.

"Now, my Irish princess," he gloated. "Let's see you ring these bells."

When he clipped those jagged babies onto my abused sensitive nipples I screamed.

Accompanying the agony was a feeling analogous to an orgasm that wracked my entire body.

It was as erotic an experience as I had ever had.

Alex seemed unfazed by my loud cry of agony/ecstasy. Apparently he was not worried that anyone else in the building might be alarmed at the keening noise.

Quite the opposite. He flashed a very contented smile on hearing my agonized cry.

"Now, Colleen," he advised me. "I want you to crawl over to Jenna and eat her cunt, but you must do so with vigor. Move so enthusiastically that those bells you're wearing will ring continuously.

"If the music you make does not please me, if, that is, it is slow and doleful, you will be punished, of course. Do you understand?"

"I will do my best to please your ears with tinkling tunes, Master, as I apply myself to regaling Jenna's twat," I informed him as I lowered my face down into the fragrant gaping hole that was so inviting.

As soon as my lips encircled Jenna's pussy-lips, she began to moan.

As I lavished kisses, licks and tongue probes around and within her hole and deep suckings to her clit, her moans transformed into groans, sighs and even giggles.

The glories experienced by my mouthings and tonguings, accompanied by Jenna's gasps and squirmings, and the joyful jingling of the bells dangling from my nipple chain, got me so excited that willy-nilly my right hand slipped down and, first gently, then fervently, twanged my own distended clit.

With a joined cry of jubilation Jenna and I uttered a violent shriek that resounded off the walls of the hot and stuffy room.

Ahh! Pure Heaven!

My bells played a roaring finale.

I fell down onto my back on the floor beside Jenna, breathing hard and trembling with delight.

Alex's angry voice cut my ecstasy short.

"Sluts!" he admonished. "Up off your backs! Now. Get onto your hands and knees and look at me adoringly."

We two submissive females snapped to it. Believe you me.

"You, Colleen," he admonished. "Did I tell you you could fluff yourself off while servicing Jenna?"

"No, you did not, Master," I acknowledged, doing my very best to look repentant.

"What do you think you deserve, then, Slut?" he asked.

"I feel I should be punished for my transgression, Master," I admitted.

My training on the Submissive Miss *was standing me in good stead.*

"How many strappings do you feel you deserve, Wench?" he asked.

"Two, Master?" I ventured.

I hoped I could get by with a minimal chastisement.

Alex arose from his chair and strode over to where I was crouching.

As he moved I kept my eyes focused adoringly on his pecker. I hoped such adulation would please him. (It happened to please me.)

He settled down on all fours in front of me and glared angrily into my eyes.

"Wrong answer, you filthy Mick bitch!" he shouted.

And with those expletives he hauled off and slapped me with such a hearty smack that it set my head to twirling and the bells suspended from my nipples to ringing a happy little tinkle-tune.

"Thank you, Master," I managed to say from somewhere within my delirium.

Alex arose and returned to his chair.

"Now, Jenna," he asked my docile companion. "How many thrashes do you think she *really* wants and deserves?"

"Eight blows seem appropriate to me, Master. She deserves them for flicking her twat when she should have been directing all her attention to my pleasure rather than her own. As per your directions, Master."

Traitor! What was wrong with the two I had suggested?

"Your answer pleases me well, Jenna," our master smiled.

"To those eight I will add eight more of my own. I desired to hear a love serenade on the wench's jangle bells while she was rummaging around in your snatch. She was too involved in her own self-abuse to ring the bells to my satisfaction.

Personally, I thought my bell ringing was most satisfactory. But I did not voice my own critique to him.

"So, Colleen the cunt, do you wish to hear what your total punishment will be?"

"I can hardly wait, Master," I told him, hoping to sound contrite enough for him to soften the blows.

"I will personally administer eight spanks to your lovely round butt. Then I will allow Jenna to follow up with eight more snaps on it with my belt."

I knew *he* would lay it on me. I hoped Jenna would be more gentle with the belt.

"You informed me that you have been spanked before by your father and others," he said.

"Yes, I have, Master," I responded truthfully.

"Then assume the position on my lap as I administer some slight little reminders to help you pay closer attention to making music when I desire a melody."

The problem I had was to position myself across his knees with my butt in the air without smashing against the massive hardon that graced the inner edge of his lap.

I somehow managed the maneuver without causing my master pain.

"I know what my function is in administering your punishment," he said. "But before I begin, you must beg me to spank you hard."

Blood was rushing to my head as my torso slumped over his well-muscled legs.

From that awkward position I managed to say, through gritted teeth:

"Please, Master. Give me a good, hard spanking."

That apparently seemed adequate to him,. Because that is exactly what he proceeded to do.

He gave me one further direction before proceeding.

"And be sure, Bitch, to count out loud the number of the swats as they land on your ass. Understand?"

"Yes, Master, I understand," I told him

I gave a start when I felt his massive hand rubbing massaging circles around my left cheek.

Ahh! I could take lots *of this!*

His palm lifted and…POW!

I cried out in pain. That *really* stung.

"ONE!" I screamed.

The sweet bastard rubbed those circles over the painful cheek again most lovingly.

God! That hurt so good.

He raised his hand.

"ZING!"

Jesus! Not only was this slap on the same abused bun. He had administered it with the back of his hand.

And those knuckles were a bitch.

"TWO!" I sobbed.

As he rubbed his knuckles over the inflamed skin I realized several things.

For the first blow, the one with his palm, his powerful biceps had given their violent force to the impact. For the second smack, the one with the knuckles, it must have been his well-developed triceps that were the power source.

And, while every blow that landed on my ass was an additional insult to my epidermis, by reversing from palm to knuckle side of his own hand, the stinging consequence to himself was cut in half.

The sneaky bastard! What a love!

So on it went, two strokes to one cheek. Then two to the other. With love-brushes from his palm that caused my cunt to cream all over his naked legs.

Oh the pain! Oh the rapture! Oh the humiliation!

When Alex had finished and I could manage to shout out "EIGHT" through my copious sobs and tears, I thanked him and managed to straighten up and get myself off my torturer's lap.

My whole attention was so directed towards the pain that tingled and throbbed at my ass that I had become totally unaware for the moment of the painful pressure my nipple chain was imposing on me.

"That was very nice, don't you think, Jenna?" Alex asked.

"Delightful, Master," she answered a bit too enthusiastically for my money.

"Now, Kate, it's time for you to beg your good friend Jenna to apply my alligator belt to your well-cured bottom."

I was still sobbing so hard that I could barely get the words out. But I managed.

"Jenna," I begged. "Would you chastise me for being so uncaring that I gave attention to my own needs rather than yours while I was eating your cunt?"

The bitch readily agreed.

Alex had me kneel in front of my chair and rest my hands and forehead in the seat while Jenna went to his chair to retrieve the rough-skinned belt that awaited her.

I kneeled there at my chair trembling, not knowing when the first wallop would slash at my exposed behind.

"PING!"

Jesus, Joseph and Mary! The girl must have been practicing flogging with a belt. She was GOOD!

"Don't forget to count!" Alex growled at me.

I did not know whether to begin counting at one or nine. I tried… "ONE!"

My response seemed to satisfy them both.

I had had my butt warmed by experts before. But those last lashes with that God damned rough belt were more than I thought I could bear.

And they were probably the most sexually satisfying moments of my life up to that point.

When I arose from my ordeal, I was mad to come. But I knew I would not be allowed the release yet.

"I believe you will do as a member of our staff, Colleen," that dreamboat Alex told me. "What do you say?"

"Thank you, Master," I replied without hesitation. "I will be happy to serve you and the director however I can."

"Well said," my master chuckled.

"Jenna will be flying to L.A. tomorrow. She will have a ticket for you, too.

"For tonight, you will stay with her at her hotel room at the Troilus Hotel. She will take you there with her now.

"Get dressed and I'll see the two of you in L.A. in a few days."

And that is how I was interviewed in New York City and came out of the experience with flying colors.

What a country I had come to.

CHAPTER FIVE

A Training Session for Summer Camp

Jenna's hotel was only three blocks away. Not at all too far to trudge while carrying my suitcase.

Jenna began our conversation by telling me how pleased she was that I got the job. She said she really liked me.

I couldn't help but ask her:

"Jenna. If you *really* like me, why did you suggest I get eight slaps rather than the two I suggested when Alex asked me?"

She laughed.

"Oh, Colleen. I'll bet you already have guessed the answer to that. Why do *you* think I did that?"

I had to laugh back.

"Because you knew that was the answer Alex expected?"

She simply nodded her head.

"And," I proceeded. "Is that why you gave me such hard slaps with the belt?"

"You're going to get along just fine at Camp Crusoe, Girlfriend," was her answer.

I knew Jenna and I were destined to be great friends.

As we walked by a bar, what we would call a pub back home, Jenna asked me if I'd like to stop in and get something to eat and drink.

I was famished, and thirsty, too.

I did not feel I had to answer and the two of us barged into the door of the place.

We sat at booth and a lively lass came over to take our order.

I looked at Jenna for an idea of what to order in this country.

"Do you like Martinis?" she asked.

"I don't know," I answered her. "I've heard of them but never tasted one."

"I'll order one for each of us, then," she decided. "We'll see if you like it. And it will be just the thing for us to toast you landing your new job."

That sounded good to me.

"She told the lass, "Two Skyy Vodka Martinis, bone dry, two olives."

The waitress flashed each of us a bright smile and wrote down the order. Before she left to get the order filled Jenna asked her:

"Do you have Buffalo wings and potato skins?"

When the lassie nodded, Jenna ordered some to go with our drinks.

When our waitress trotted off with the order, I had to ask Jenna, "Do the buffalos in America really have wings?"

She burst out laughing.

"Buffalo is the name of a city up-state. A bar up there came up with a method of cooking chicken wings. I think you'll like them."

Well, I had a lot to learn about the country I'd ended up in.

When the drinks arrived, I took a sip of my Martini.

"Why, Jenna!" I exclaimed. "It's just cold vodka with a couple of olives in it."

"Of course," she answered. "But do you like it?"

"Love it," I answered truthfully.

We exchanged toasts with each sip.

"To your new job." "To America." "To Buffalo." "To Catalina." "To men with trim bums." "To you," "And back to you."

By the time the waitress had returned with our food order, we had toasted our way halfway through the icy gin.

The Buffalo wings were delicious. And I thought I'd eaten potatoes prepared every way possible back in County Cork. But the skins, loaded with cheese, bacon and other things were just wonderful.

Could it be the Martinis that made each dish seem so tasty and wonderful?

As we ate, we finished our Martinis and ordered a second round. As we nibbled and drank we discussed what we had done with each other at my interview.

I admitted to her that I had never kissed a girl before.

"It's just like kissing a boy. But different," Jenna commented.

I thought that was hilarious and the two of us hugged each other as we gave in to our mirth – and to the influence of our drinks.

I had a hard time managing to bring up the subject of how much I had enjoyed the cunnilingus and the pleasure of our mutual orgasm. But, somehow the gin seemed to help me broach and elaborate on the subject.

She told me the practice is called "muff diving."

That brought a new rash of laughter to our booth.

The other customers in the pub – bar – did not appear upset at our rowdy behavior.

By the time we had finished off the food and drinks we were even laughing about the spanking and the whipping I'd received.

When she told me how much fun she'd had tanning my hide with Alex's belt, I admitted that it had turned me on, too. And that I was looking forward to whipping her bum in return the first chance I got.

I let her pay the bill when we were through.

And hand in hand, we strolled on down the street to the Troilus Hotel and our room.

The first thing I noticed when we entered the room was that it only had one bed. A double one.

As I stood up after placing my suitcase on the floor in a corner I saw that Jenna was disrobing.

Completely.

As I watched her luscious body appear out of her clothing I felt a clench in my cleft, remembering the great spasm I'd experienced as I "dove into her muff" as the Americans put it.

In the back of my mind I was hoping that I might find an occasion to re-live that experience.

Even though Jenna and I had been deeply sexually involved during my interview with Alex, I felt bashful about following her lead there in the hotel room. So I hesitated getting out of own clothes.

But the Martinis I'd indulged in so recently helped me overcome my inhibitions and I was soon getting myself as comfortably naked as my roommate.

With my head still spinning pleasantly from the alcohol, I flopped my bare-assed self down onto the bed.

I smiled a conspiratorial smile as I became aware of Jenna settling down next to me.

She leaned over me and pressed her lips to mine.

I did not resist the move. Rather, I met her tongue with my own in a titillating exchange.

As we were thus orally engaged, one of Jenna's hands cupped my right tit. I gladly welcomed it there.

As she pulled, pinched and rubbed my nipples I responded in kind. My hands busily teased her nipples in as many ways as she was playing with mine.

Even though this was my first time in a romantic situation in bed with another girl, the situation did not seem unnatural in the least to me.

Jenna lay back down flat on her back and rested her hand on my pubis.

I lay there, hands behind my head, staring blankly at the ceiling, enjoying the sensations that bubbled up and down my body.

"You know what?" I asked my companion.

"What?" she answered as she traced a wanton finger over my slit.

"I sure loved those Martinis," I blurted.

We both giggled like little girls.

"You know what?" she said to me.

"No, what," I responded.

"We have to get you shaved," she said seriously.

"None of the chicks on the staff at camp are allowed to wear pussy-beards."

A revelation.

So, just as I was beginning to get nice and moist down in my crotch, Jenna hopped out of bed, went into the bathroom and returned with her electric razor.

She slipped a towel under my bum to catch the harvest of pubic hair.

The razor was the kind that has a trimmer. She turned it on and trimmed my bush very carefully. What a sensation that was. Particularly as she got down to the area around my mound.

Then, when the forest was cleaned off she switched to the razor function of the machine and I got a whole new batch of exciting sensations.

I was getting a new buzz. A kind of buzz on top of a buzz.

When she'd finished with me she ran a hand over my now bald pubis and pussy.

Whee!

I slipped my hand under hers and ran a course over the new-mowed area.

Did *that* ever get the juices to flowing!

Next, it was my turn to shave her.

There was no need for the trimmer function of the implement on her pubis. There was only stubble on my new girlfriend's twat. But using the razor on it got me really hot. And the moisture gathering at her crotch gave testimony that she was getting more and more turned on all the time.

When I had finished with her, she and I were each rubbing our hands over the results of my handiwork.

The New World was certainly offering me new experiences I had never previously even imagined.

Jenna got off the bed with the towel holding the harvest of my short-curlies. She emptied the towel in the bathroom and returned with two damp washcloths.

"Let's clean ourselves up down there before we play games, huh? Do you want to play games?"

I had no idea what she had in mind. But I did know I was fully into the mood to follow Jenna's lead into whatever she meant by "games."

We each sat up on the bed wiping our cunts and our assholes clean.

In the case of the cunt area, we were both sopping with our own juices.

And the fragrance from that area was more intoxicating even than the effects left over from the lunch Martinis.

When we were well mopped up down below, Jenna carried our washcloths back to the bathroom and returned to our bed with a bunch of ropes.

We propped ourselves up against the headboard, looked at each other, and had a good laugh.

"All right, Jenna," I asked. "What's next?"

"Have you ever experienced bondage?" she asked me with a wicked smile on her face.

I gave her a short review of my experiences at Ballycormac and aboard the Submissive Miss.

"Would you like to get bound here in our room and have some real fun, Girlfriend? Just us two girls?" she inquired.

"Let's go for it...Girlfriend," I told her with very positive anticipation.

"You're not only going to enjoy this," my newly acquired girlfriend assured me. "You'll benefit by learning to cope with some of the practices that await us over on Catalina."

"Do me, then," I told her.

And we were still sufficiently under the influence of the Martinis to think that was funny enough to warrant an exchange of giggles.

I saw that the ropes were all about the same length.

She took one of the shorter ropes in hand and had me look at it closely.

"This is a rope made of pure cotton fibers," she told me. "If you're ever inclined to go out and buy rope for fun and games, cotton is usually the best choice. When I buy rope for bed bondage I get twelve foot lengths. That seems to work for most beds.

"There is a nylon webbing that Zach likes to use, but for most of us cotton twisted rope does the trick just fine."

I hoped that I would be able to remember that later because I was pretty sure I would be wanting bondage rope sometime in the future when I would want to invite a companion to enjoy a bit of bondage with me.

"Now, spread out flat on your back here on the bed," Jenna ordered.

"Spread-eagle your arms and legs reaching toward the four corners of the bed."

That was easy enough.

"You're a little bit tense, Colleen," she told me. "You've got to relax more."

I tried to let go of the tension I was feeling. But all this was new to me and I have to admit I was pretty excited.

"Now, give me one of your hands," she said.

She folded the rope in half and put the half-way spot on the pulse-point on my wrist. Then she looped the rope three times around my wrist.

"Is that too tight?" she asked.

I'd been cuffed enough before to be able to judge what it should feel like and I told her she had me cuffed just fine.

"Now," she explained. "I'm tying the rope together here at your wrist in a square knot. Do you know how to tie a square knot?"

I had to admit that I wasn't sure.

"No problem," she declared. "After I release you and you tie me up, it will work out all right with nearly any old knot. But before we get to camp I'll have to teach you how to tie the knot right. You'll be expected to know how to do that."

I shook my head in agreement.

"The next step is the tuck," she told me. "When you tie your shoes, do you ever make the extra tuck at the end to secure the knot?"

I told her I always tucked in my knots.

She looped the rope into a tuck.

"There," she exclaimed. "One cuff done. When it's your turn to do me, do you feel you can get me cuffed like that?"

It was, of course, a no brainer. And I told her so.

"Good, then," she continued. "Now relax this arm back down on the bed where it was before, take a deep breath and relax even more than last time."

I found it easy to relax pretty much all the way as Jenna tied the two ends of the rope securely to the headboard. As she did so she mentioned that the tie up there was a square knot, too. I got the point.

She then cuffed and secured my other arm in the same way without needing to explain what she was doing.

Now that I was rope-handcuffed and bound to the headboard, my arms extended in a Y, I knew without having to be told that the next step was to be footcuffed and secured to the footboard. So I willed myself to relax fully while Jenna wrapped me and tugged at the ropes until I was bound so I was incapable of even squirming very much. I told her so.

"Yep," she declared, looking over the job she'd done on me. "You sure enough are trussed up like a Christmas turkey."

That set both of us to laughing again.

And, as I had discovered at Ballycormac and aboard the Submissive Miss, bondage, of and by itself, is a gigantic turn-on.

"How does that feel?" Jenna asked me.

"Terrific!" I enthused.

"You're going to love Catalina, then, Girl," she assured me.

"Now, do you know how to breathe without panicking during a bum-kiss and a deep-throat?"

I told her I didn't even know what she was talking about.

"I kind of thought that might be the case," she told me. "I don't want you to experience either of those unprepared. So let's get with it," she explained.

"First, the bum-kiss.

"To start off, you need to be sure you're securely tied down enough that you can't squirm away from me no matter what I do to you."

I assured her that I was as trussed up as the turkey she'd described.

And, again, we both burst out laughing.

"Now," she said when we were over our giggles.

"I'd better tell you what a bum-kiss is. It's pretty much exactly what it sounds like. You are going to kiss my ass.

"Not any old kiss, mind you. It has to be a French kiss.

"One of the reasons we cleaned up our assholes with the washcloths was for this particular game. So get ready."

I have to admit that the idea did not appeal to me much. Then I remembered that I had been "tongue-fucked" on board ship, probably by Bates, while the captain was whisking my titties.

What an experience *that* had been.

Having experienced the elation I felt then gave me an entirely new prospect on the bum-kiss.

"Let's do it," I invited Jenna.

She positioned herself above me, a knee on each side of my waist, and facing the footboard.

She scooted backward until her backsides were poised directly over my face.

"Now, Colleen," she said. "I'm going to spread my cheeks as wide as I can get them. You'll be looking up at my rosy little asshole. When I lower myself down, I'm aiming it at your mouth.

"That will, of course, cut off your breathing. Now the trick is for you to make a point of the end of your tongue and insert it into the hole as you take a big breath. When you pull your tongue out, I will lift myself up. As I lower my butt back down, you kiss the hole and give me tongue again. When we get our rhythm going, you won't be panicking about breathing at all. And if you don't begin to cream on the covers underneath you while we're doing this number, I miss my bet."

It took me a few probes to get into the spirit of the thing. But then, as I remembered Bates tongue-fucking my ass as the pain was wrenching my nipples, I got so excited I actually wondered if I would come if we continued this for long.

As it turned out, the butt-kiss was a fairly short session because as I was to find out at a later date when I was the top, it's pretty exhausting to do the rising-falling bit.

When Jenna got her butt out of my face she sat down on the bed next to me.

"How did that go for you?" she asked, out of breath.

"It was an experience," I had to admit, somewhat out of breath myself.

"Now," she told me. "One more breathing exercise and then we'll have a different kind of fun.

"Deep-throat is not real pleasant at first. Not for the bottom anyway. When the top is a guy with a loaded prick, it clearly is a great experience for him.

"Deep-throat is exactly what it sounds like. It's a lot like sucking cock, but you don't really suck."

"I don't get it," I told her.

"No, but you *will*!" Jenna smiled that wicked smile she unleashed from time to time.

She got off the bed and went over to the dresser and brought out a dildo.

Oh-oh!

I had an uncomfortable feeling about what might be in store for me next.

She held the object up where I could get a good look at it.

It was not a particularly big phallus. But I found it quite attractive. It was not as long as Jamie O'Doul's darling prick. And it certainly had a smaller circumference than his. But it was of sufficient magnitude to satisfy any sex act I could imagine.

"I call this one my training dildo," Jenna told me.

"You don't want your first experience practicing deep-throat with a guy to be with some great big dick slamming into your throat. This jobbie is going to be large enough to break you into the practice.

"The top will be a guy who is going to get at least the tip of his bulb down into your throat. Some fellows will pound until the whole helmet has been swallowed.

"Your gag reaction will set in immediately. That's what the dudes like. That gagging gives their pricks the ultimate erotic massage.

"The tricky thing for you, as the bottom, is to find a way to breathe while your throat is stopped up. And the only way to do that is through your nose.

"So what you have to do right now is open your mouth so I can insert this baby in."

It was with some apprehension that I accepted that darling representation of a prick into my mouth.

"Now," Jenna advised me. "Suck the bulb there as it enters your mouth. Give it a good working over with your lips. Suck deep on it. And flicker your tongue over the piss-hole. I'm sure you've given enough head to know what guys like. Even in practice like this, give it all you've got."

I have to admit that sucking that thing got me to dampening my groin. The little thing was so cute. And the favorite cock I'd ever sucked, Jamie's, came to mind quite vividly as I give the dildo my all.

Sucking while in full bondage restraint gave a dimension to the action that was particularly sensual. In other words, I was having myself a time while sucking a lovely piece of plastic.

"Now," Jenna advised me. "I'm going to let you suck this baby deeper into your mouth. Slurp in so that the sensitive ridge is beyond your teeth. That's it. Give a little special treatment to the ridge itself. That drives the boys nuts. They are always grateful when a girl gives it a lascivious tongue swirl.

"Now, I'm going to slip this baby back and forth so you can give that ridge everything you've got. Get your top to moaning and groaning as you pleasure his cock helmet."

I was getting into it big time now. I squirmed around against my restraints and my pussy lips were clenching and unclenching with lust. Oh how those lips would welcome a cock. But, since the cock was up in my face, my mouth lips got to mimic my nether ones.

So the dildo gradually got inserted farther and farther into my oral cavity.

"Remember now," Jenna told me. "You're breathing through your nose now. Just keep doing so. Relax and enjoy the sensation. But keep breathing."

I was breathing and pulling against my restrains and sucking and squirming and smiling and…

Oops! Gag time.

I gagged violently as that dildo got dangerously close to my throat opening. My whole body revolted.

"Great!" Jenna encouraged me. "That's a terrific gag response. The dudes will love it!"

Well, I can tell you *I* did not love it.

Breathe, breathe, breathe, I told myself as that damned fake prick hit the opening to my throat.

My body spasmed, tears ran down my cheeks. I felt a panic attack.

Jenna pulled the damned thing out of my mouth.

"Not bad for the first time," she assured me. "All of us gals on the staff at camp have learned to do it. And we all love it. You will too once you get used to it."

I wasn't so sure. And the experience had left me confused and inarticulate.

Well, that first trial was not the end of the session. Jenna repeated inserting that thing into my mouth and back into my throat until I managed to actually get the head fully into my throat.

When she pulled it out of my mouth following that accomplishment she told me:

"You did swell, Babe. I'm going to leave this dildo over here on the dresser for you. It's up to you to practice with it on your own now. If you want to keep your job, you'll have to learn to swallow it and love doing so. You'll make it, I'm sure."

I wasn't so sure myself at the time
But then, I told myself, "Jenna probably knows best."
And I left it at that for the moment.

Jenna released my bonds from the headboard and footboard. But the cuffs remained on my wrists and ankles.

"Break time!" she announced.

"I have a bottle of Chardonnay in the mini-fridge and some cheese and crackers." she added.

I responded enthusiastically. A wine and cheese party after my bondage experiences seemed quite welcome.

And, since I was still trailing ropes from my arms and legs, I knew that following our break I had another round of bondage practice to go through.

The wine was cool and refreshing. And I'd worked up a bit of hunger during my experiences as a bottom with a female domina.

We took a good half-hour break when Jenna informed me it was time for Part Two of our game.

"How many parts are there?" I asked.

She laughed.

"Just two for you as a bottom. After our next round you get to tie me up, be the top, and do whatever the Hell you want with me."

I practically drooled as visions of dominating Jenna flitted through my mind.

I wasn't real sure I was up to another "training session" yet. But I realized that when "Part Two" was over, I'd get a chance to play the domina, the top, the one who called the shots.

That would be a first for me. And something worth enduring one more session for.

"Stretch out on the bed on your tummy this time, Girlfriend," Jenna ordered.

As I stretched out, face down, I extended my arms and legs towards the four corners of the bed. There was no need to be told the drill. I got it the first time.

Jenna had me trussed up in a trice. She was a girl who certainly knew the ropes.

The whole feeling of bondage when face down on a bed contrasts markedly with its counterpart. I discovered that whether my nose was burrowing down into the bed's surface or my neck was twisted so I was pressing an ear down, I was quite uncomfortable.

And the pressure on my boobs against the flat surface left something to be desired in the comfort department as well.

Then came the next indignity.

Slap!

Jenna had given me a very sharp slap to my bare exposed ass.

I had been spanked by Daddy and by Alex before, of course. And I guess I had accepted the punishment as a male prerogative.

And Jenna had whipped me with a belt at my interview. But that was different from this.

A bare female hand spanking my vulnerable butt aroused a whole new set of sensations within me.

And, I have to admit, the sensations were not disagreeable.

There were only four hand spanks, two to each bun. And they stung.

With each smack, Jenna went through the seemingly required rebukes about me being naughty, a slut, and so on. Those repetitions seemed to me to satisfy the spanker more than the spankee. I had learned to ignore them back in my childhood.

My backsides were, I know, pinkish from the light spanking. And they tingled delightfully.

And I felt a satisfaction in knowing that Jenna's delicate feminine hand was as pinkish and as tingly as my own rear end.

But when she went to the closet and came back with a wooden coat hanger, I knew I was really in for it.

"I detected one of your secrets at your interview this morning," Jenna revealed to me spanking the palm of her left hand with a resounding smack.

"What secret might that be, Dearie?" I asked, half-aware of what she would proclaim.

"I vividly remember you slumped across Alex's knees, your bare ass pointed up at the ceiling.

"And I distinctly remember you saying, "Please, Master. Give me a good hard spanking."

"That's what Alex ordered me to say," I answered indignantly, aware she was on to something. "So what?"

"I understood the meaning behind your statement. You really meant it, didn't you?"

"No, I didn't!" I objected.

Whack!

That hanger came down with such a hard snap that I knew it raised a welt on my sensitive bottom.

"Liar!" Jenna shouted as I cried out in pain.

"You loved it, didn't you? Go ahead. Admit it!"

"It hurt. It stung. I hated it," I remonstrated.

Zing!

God Almighty! That one landed right on top of the other blow. I knew I now had a welt on my welt. And an even more painful one than the first.

"Stop it!" I protested. "You're hurting me, Jenna."

I was crying hard now.

"There was pain when Alex spanked you, wasn't there? Excruciating pain," she exulted.

Smack!

Through my sobs, tears and protests I was able to articulate:

"It hurt like what you're doing to me now, Jenna. Please stop it!"

"Feel the pain, Bitch," she laughed. "Feel the humiliation! Feel the clench in your twat. Feel your juices draining out of you and onto the sheets!"

She knew! Jenna *did* know my secret.

"You love it, don't you, Slut?"

Wham!

"You're so turned on you're about to come right now! Aren't you?" she exulted.

"Yes, yes, yes," I cried out."

"I felt I had to come back at the interview," I admitted to her. "And I'm mad to come now. Right now! Finger fuck me, Jenna. Now! Please!"

Jenna laughed.

And I had to laugh along with her. Because I knew that she knew what I knew about her at that moment. I was totally aware that she was absolutely as masochistic as I am. She loved to be spanked, too.

Jenna loved a good spanking every bit as much as I did.

But, Jenna maintained her pose of domina still. For the moment.

"You don't get to come yet, my dear. No, no. Not yet. There's still another little game we're going to play while you're bound up face down on the sheets."

I wondered what she had in store for me next.

She took that lovely brutal hanger back to the closet. Then, from the dresser drawer she took out an object. I could not make out what it was.

She brought it over to the bed and held it out for me to see.

What in the world is that thing?" I asked.

"This?" she asked archly. "It's only a butt-plug. Haven't you ever seen one before?"

It was clear that I had not.

It was about three inches long, bulb-shaped at the top with a flared base. The long bulb was ridged. It was made of some kind of red plastic.

Jenna was lubricating the bulb with Astrolube.

"Your ass is so flushed and shiny," she said, rubbing a hand caressingly over each of my moons.

Ow!

"Hurts so good, doesn't it, Girlfriend?" Jenna said lovingly.

"Stop! Don't stop!" was my answer.

"With a nice hot ass, there's nothing more satisfying than an ass-fuck with a butt-plug," Jenna assured me.

"A dildo up the ass can be dangerous," she told me. "If it slips up out of control you can be, literally, in deep shit. With this flare at the base of the plug, the little devil can't go scurrying off into your bowels.

"And these little ridges you see all around the bulb? Just you wait until you feel them hippidy-hop as they caress your asshole!"

With that introduction, Jenna spread my cheeks apart, slipped the well-lubricated narrow head of the plug into my hole and ran that plug in and out of the channel with loads of loving care.

My God, it felt wonderful. It made me cream and cream and cream.

"Some of the guys really go for the bottom wearing one of these babies up the ass while they're fucking you," she told me. "They can feel those ridges against their pricks as they're thrusting up and down. You want to have one handy to please the ones who dig that," she informed me.

I was finding out that I get a kick out of having an ass-plug in me. Another new discovery.

"I need an orgasm, Jenna!" I screamed. "Now!"

"Not yet," she cooed as she unbound me completely.

"I want us to come together. After you've bound, humiliated and tortured me. It'll be worth the wait."

Well, now another new experience awaited me. Since I was a little girl, I had always been the one to be hit, beaten and humiliated. Jenna was going to give me a chance to see what it was like at the "dishing out" end.

She handed me the four ropes. And with them I tied her up the way I had observed her do me.

Three circles of the wrists. Make a knot.

I didn't know whether my knot was "square" or not. And Jenna didn't comment. After all, I was the top on this round, not her.

But the knot held. And she'd promised to teach me the right way before we got to camp.

After successfully cuffing her wrists I did her ankles.

Somehow I drew great satisfaction just cuffing someone for the first time.

I decided that for my first try at submitting another person to my will I'd just start by binding Jenna to the bed face down.

Most of all, I wanted to spank her. What a rare treat that would be for me.

Then, I was intrigued with the butt-plug. So I wanted to fool around with that precious toy.

Then, I planned to turn her over and "muff dive" her.

I knew that "doing" her those three ways would satisfy my need to learn to be in charge in this bondage game.

I raised my right hand over Jenna's shapely ass and came down with a resounding slap.

Ow!

The cry of pain was mine, not hers. I'd left a red mark on her bum, all right. And I imagined it stung.

But my palm was as red as her cheek. And stung like Hell, too.

Jenna giggled and I boiled.

"Damn it," I cursed. "That hurt!"

"Cry baby," Jenna taunted.

Wait a minute. Here I was supposed to be the top and I was being mocked by my bottom.

Not fair!

I decided that spanking a bottom with my bare hand was not my thing at all. And I was quite angry with Jenna for her teasing response to my humiliation at intimating "this hurts me more than it hurts you."

I marched myself to the closet and took down a hefty wooden hanger.

"You're going to get it now, Girl," I growled at Jenna. "Make fun of my stinging palm, will you? You're going to pay for that!"

I was surprised at my vehemence. And at the satisfaction gave me to express it.

I raised the hanger above Jenna's ass and came down with a resounding whack.

The welt it left had nearly drawn blood.

Jenna let out a cry that I thought might be heard over on Times Square.

"God, Colleen," she sobbed. "You don't need to be so brutal!"

"Brutal am I?" I snarled back at her. "I've hardly begun tanning your sluttish hide. Take *that*, Bitch!"

And the force I put into that next slap surprised even me.

I had that girl howling and begging for mercy as I continued to vent my spleen, recalling all the times I had been spanked and flogged.

Someone had to pay for the years I had suffered the beatings and humiliation. And Jenna happened to be the recipient of my pent up wrath.

The slapping sound I was making was music to my ears. The rippling of Jenna's prime tender flesh was a glory to my eyes.

At last I knew the feeling of power that Daddy, McCarthy, Captain O'Sullivan, Alex and most recently Jenna had felt.

Glorious!

When I was through, I had not drawn any blood. But I had drawn tears, sobs, shrieks and moans.

The power rush I felt made a beeline right down into my pounding cunt. The throbbing there was just unbelievable.

"Now, Cunt," I advised Jenna. "If you apologize for taunting me when I gave you the first hand spank, I may, just *may* give you only one more strike with this instrument."

"I'm sorry. I'm sorry," Jenna wailed.

"Say, 'I humbly beg your forgiveness, Mistress,'" I commanded. And landed a good stripe on her butt.

"Ouch! I humbly beg your forgiveness, Mistress," my newly acquired slave sobbed.

I'd gotten my repressed frustrations out of my system and left my girlfriend stretched out on the bed, crying her eyes out as I took the hanger back to the closet.

And as I returned to the bedside I knew that Jenna had relished the beating I had given her absolutely as much as I had enjoyed administering it.

"Did you have a good time, Jenna?" I teased her.

"Oh, just lovely, Mistress," she answered. "I just don't know how to thank you enough."

"I couldn't be more pleased, myself," I informed her.

It may have come across as an ironic answer. But, in actuality, it was sincere.

"On my way back here to the bed from returning the hanger to the closet, I picked up this sweet little toy," I informed her. "And I absolutely could not resist bringing it back here to see whether it will continue to amuse."

I held out the butt-plug for her to see.

"Oh, goodie, goodie," Jenna enthused.

I rubbed a hand over her buns ever so lightly. And she clenched her cleft as her blushing buns sent shivers of delightful pain into her very core.

"Now, My Dear," I told her. "I have to take a gander at that rosy rectum your clinging moons are concealing. Bashful?"

"Oh, not at all, Mistress," Jenna answered. "My asshole is all yours. Please feel free."

I did, of course, feel quite free.

I laid the plug on the bed and took hold on each side of her butt-crack and opened up the way to her pink treasure.

My inquisitive eye was confronted with a little pink bud that all but winked at me. I had, of course, had quite an introduction to it as it had repeatedly descended on my face for the butt-kiss when I was the bottom and she was the top.

I could not help myself. I spit on my index finger and rubbed the puckered little bugger.

The sphincter recoiled.

Oh, fun!

I slipped the tip of my finger into the hole.

Jenna pressed down, clenching my fingertip.

Whee!

I took my finger out, covered the plug with the lube and placed the tip of the implement on the surface of her expectant hole.

And I pleasured that sweetheart's anus in, out, farther in, partial withdrawal…

Did I ever give her asshole a royal fucking.

She moaned in delight. But she was not the only one purring. She was creaming the sheets something fierce. But not any more-so than I was.

When we were each aroused to a very high point, I had to reverse her bondage.

Setting the plug aside, I untied the ropes at the head-and footboards and ordered my victim/my toy to turn over, face up. I then secured her again to the boards.

Once she was firmly secured, I buried my face in that girl's cunt and lapped away like a mamma lioness licking her cub.

When she was twitching on the point of orgasm I reversed my position, remembered the sixty-nine thing Jamie O'Doul and I had accomplished at the pool at Ballycormac and Jenna and I brought each other off with tongue action that left us both breathless and in spasms.

I untied my girlfriend from her restraints and flopped down beside her.

We laughed and giggled so you would have thought we were barmy.

And fell into a deep, satisfying sleep with our fingers in each other's cunts.

And that was my first day in America.
And the most educational day I had ever had up until then.

CHAPTER SIX

Hollywood Daze

I had never flown on an airplane before. You would think that flying from New York to Los Angeles would have been an exciting prospect for a simple Irish lass like myself.

But I guess I had been through enough experiences since my introduction to Headmaster McCarthy's "chamber" to make as commonplace a matter as being transported for three thousand miles at thirty-five thousand feet above the earth's surface no big deal.

At the New York airport I simply followed Jenna. She had our tickets and identification cards. I couldn't tell what she laid on the counter for my identity card. Later she showed it to me. It was, surprisingly, a California driver's license with my picture and my name on it.

Imagine!

What kind of people was I working for?

The flight was uneventful. Jenna and I were seatmates, but we did not talk much. I read some articles in the airline magazine in the seat pocket in front of me. I was hoping there would be information about Los Angeles or Catalina. But instead the articles were singularly uninteresting and unhelpful.

When we landed in Los Angeles Jenna and I took a taxi to someplace called West Hollywood.

I had a mental picture of what Hollywood would look like. Sparkling. Glamorous. Full of movie stars driving around in convertibles.

My illusions were shattered. West Hollywood is, I discovered, a very nice neighborhood of Los Angeles. But it is not any more glamorous than nice neighborhoods in County Cork.

The taxi took us to the Motel Defoe on Santa Monica Boulevard.

Jenna had told me on the way there that the motel belonged to our boss-man, Zachary Lund. And that it was where his employees could stay rent-free when in the Los Angeles area.

She told me she and I would be roommates there, which did not surprise me. And that our room had a Pullman kitchen, but that it was not of sufficient capacity to prepare most of our meals.

We would be eating out during most of our Hollywood stay.

On the plane, she'd told me that our stop in L.A. (that's what she called Los Angeles) and Hollywood would only be for a week or so. It was to be our stopover before catching a boat to Catalina Island.

At the motel office a nice young lady told us we were expected and gave Jenna a key to Room Seven.

It appeared that one key would suffice for the two of us.

Fine with me.

Room Seven did not appear unusual in any way from the exterior.

And when Jenna opened the door to the room, I noticed immediately that not only one key would suffice for us. One bed would, as well. A nice spacious king sized four-poster bed awaited our arrival.

I smiled at her and she smiled back.

It was nice to have a girlfriend.

When we had entered our room, I saw that it had some rather unusual features.

For one, each of the four posts at the corners of the bed had four eyebolts spaced along it, with a fifth eyebolt at the top.

There were also eyebolts on the headboard and footboard.

I looked up at the ceiling and was surprised to see a large mirror mounted up there, with the same dimensions as the bed itself. My reflection was gazing down at me.

The room reminded me of two rooms I had been in previously. Two rooms that had made deep impressions on me.

One was Headmaster McCarthy's "chamber." And the other was Captain O'Sullivan's "chapel."

Like the Ballycormac chamber, there were pulleys installed on the ceiling with ropes running through them. Hanging from one suspended rope was a large, sturdy hook.

Hmm. Familiar.

From another pulley hung a trapeze bar.

The other attachments were a mystery to me, which I did not feel like exploring at the time.

Occupying the room's western wall was a Saint George's Cross. The kind of cross that sits on its side, forming an X.

What a novel fixture for a motel room.

I further noticed that there were eyebolts at the ends of each of the two criss-crossed boards of the cross.

Further inspection of the room revealed many more eyebolts scattered around the walls. *Hmmm!*

This motel room clearly was not decorated as a stop-over for the average tourist who came to Hollywood to visit movie studios or to see the homes of the stars.

When I realized what the room really was designed for, I dampened my panties.

I could see party time ahead.

The last object that drew my attention was an old-fashioned locked steamer trunk.

I pointed it out to Jenna and asked her what the container was for.

"Oh, that," she informed me. "That old trunk contains a few of Zack's implements."

From the smile she shot me I could easily imagine that some of the "implements" in that chest were capable of inflicting pain.

I wondered if I would ever find out in a personal way.

When we were unpacked and had our clothes hung up in the closet and tucked into drawers, I asked Jenna to tell me a bit about our boss, Zack.

"I think you'll like him," she told me. "He's quite imposing, you know. He's tall, strong and muscular. Somewhere in his late thirties or early forties. Ruggedly handsome and…hung like a stallion."

That last bit of gratuitous information made me blush and then giggle right along with her.

"He's a mover and shaker here in Hollywood," she continued.

"He has all kinds of contacts with people in the industry."

I was wise enough to know she meant the entertainment industry.

"He has his fingers in more pies than I can imagine," she elaborated.

"Among other things, he caters to some of the kinkier foibles of the rich and famous. If you look around the room you can guess what some of those are.

"The campers who are sent to Camp Crusoe are the kids of the top executives and performers in the industry. There's no 'funny business' with the campers. We provide good, wholesome fun and activities for them. You'll love working with the youngsters.

"There are a few spoiled brats, of course. But most our campers are just plain good kids. Rich kids, it's true. But essentially just normal fun-living kids.

"But the staff is another matter. Zack is a control freak. And whoever he hires for any of his enterprises must be absolutely submissive to him.

"But here I am going on and on. And we have places to go and things to do.

"Like eat. I'm starving. How about you?"

She hit the right button on that one. I was famished.

Jenna knew the bus routes in the area and there was a bus stop right at one of the corners near the motel.

She had a favorite restaurant on Melrose she took me to and we got a window table.

Over lunch Jenna told me that after we'd eaten we had to go shop for the swimsuit I'd be wearing at camp. And then we'd pay an exploratory trip to T4T.

I asked her what T4T was.

"It's a store that sells BDSM equipment," she told me.

The blank look on my face was enough to tell her I did not know what she was talking about.

"BDSM," she repeated. "Bondage, discipline, sadism and masochism. It is the lifestyle of all of us who are Zack's employees…his slaves. You must have figured out back in New York that you were hired for the Catalina job because you clearly fit in with the staff."

I had not previously known the designation of BDSM. But I certainly was aware that I had experienced the lifestyle.

My experiences at McCarthy's hands in Ireland. What the crew on the boat coming to America inflicted on me. Those experiences fit the four letters B.D.S.M.

In a sense, even my relationship with Daddy had elements of submission, sadism and masochism.

I had learned since arriving in the New World that I get off on inflicting pain. And all my life I had responded pleasantly viscerally to being subjected and being punished.

Wow! Brave new world that has such people in it.

The next place we visited after lunch was a sporting goods store.

When we entered, an attractive young lady clerk approached us and greeted Jenna by name.

I was introduced to the attendant.

"Jill. This is Colleen, the newest member of the Camp Crusoe staff. She will be working with Jason in the swimming and water sports program."

Whoa!? Jason? Nobody had told me about any Jason.

"It's nice to meet you, Colleen," Jill greeted me. "Jason is just darling. Have you met him yet? No?

"You'll like him. So I suppose you're here to pick up your swimsuit."

I supposed that was what I was there for, so dumbly nodded my head.

Jill sized me up and down with her eyes and disappeared into a back room.

She returned with a black unitard swimsuit with the words STAFF CAMP ROBINSON CRUSOE emblazoned on the top.

Jill invited me to try it on in the changing room.

It fit me perfectly.

Knowing now a lot more about what to expect when I got to Catalina, I realized that the unitard would hide any bruises, welts, slash marks or other evidence of whippings I was likely to endure on Catalina.

I returned to the display room in the unitard. The two girls made approving comments on how I looked in it.

I asked what my co-worker, Jason, would be wearing while we were working. I couldn't help but wonder how a male swimsuit could cover over the lashes I knew the whole staff would be bearing.

From Jenna's wicked smile I could tell she divined the reason for my request.

Jill excused herself, went back to the stockroom and returned with a male two-piece swimsuit. The top was a lycra rashguard with the same lettering displayed on it as on my unitard.

I could see that none of our young charges in the water program would ever catch sight of the telltale marks that their counselors, male or female, bore surreptitiously under our uniforms.

I returned to the dressing room, changed back into my street clothes, and handed my "uniform" back to Jill.

I was informed that the purchase would be put on Mister Lund's account.

We thanked Jill and trudged out to go to the mysterious T4T shop.

On the bus to our next stop, Jenna asked me about what my attitudes were toward gays and lesbians.

The question threw me a bit. Because I had never given much thought to the matter. I had enjoyed engaging in sexual activities with her. But I wouldn't attach the word "lesbian" to our frolics. After all, it was males who really had always rung my bell. And still did.

I knew there were guys who liked guys. And the crew members on the *Submissive Miss* handled each other's peters. But I would hardly label them "gay."

I told Jenna, truthfully, that I had no attitude towards anything that one person did with another, or with others, sexually.

"The reason I asked," Jenna told me. "Is that the salesman, Cary, at our next stop, the T4T, is not only gay. He's a flaming gay. A femme. He's heavily muscled, and quite good looking, but he flits about the place in a very effeminate way and speaks with girlish inflections. I wanted to warn you in case you are homophobic."

I did not know the term homophobic. But it was obvious to me what it meant.

Effeminate men and masculine women had never affected me one way or another. And I told Jenna that she needn't be concerned about how I might react to Cary the salesperson.

When we got off the bus and were walking toward the store I asked Jenna what the T4T stood for.

She laughed.

"As I told you, it's a boutique for BDSM items. You might say it's a toy store. There are BDSM toys on sale there, along with clothes that some adepts wear, whips, fetish toys, what have you. You'll see the kinds of things they sell as soon as you enter the door. The T4T has different meanings for different people, I guess. For some, it could mean 'Toys for Tarts.' Or 'Toys for Twats.' Certainly 'Toys for Torture' fits the bill.

"About the only thing I can think of that doesn't fit is 'Tea for Two.'

Her answer satisfied my curiosity.

As we approached the store, I was not too surprised to see that the door and the window facing the street were opaque. The reason why seemed clear enough to me. The displays inside would probably be offensive to some pedestrians passing by.

When we entered, I was not shocked.

On open display on the walls, in display cases and on tables there were all kinds of whips, paddles, cuffs, ropes, masks, dildoes and restraints.

And scores of items whose uses I could not fathom in the least.

On one of the bare walls, there were silhouettes of full-sized human forms, male and female.

In addition to the silhouettes there were targets of varying sizes and heights.

Free-standing in the area were several manikins. They bore signs of having been subjected to target practice.

I knew immediately that the wall was a testing site for whips.

I was drawn to the display cases over by the testing area. I found I was enthralled by the assortment of pain inflicting instruments. The sight tickled my long suppressed lust to inflict pain.

I gazed from one luscious instrument to the next. Each one was labeled with its own name – names that I learned to love at first sight.

"Single lash whip, whipsickle, latigo, bullwhip, buggywhip, riding crop, blacksnake, rattan cane, hickory stick, birch rod, truncheon, paddle, frat bat, strap, slapper…"

Did you ever see such a panty-soaking list of words before in your entire life?

And those were only a few of the names that designated the cunt-clenching objects themselves.

I was so wrapped up in greedily visually devouring the floggers that I was unaware of the approach of the salesman.

I suddenly felt his presence when an enthusiastic high-pitched voice assailed my ears.

"Aren't they absolutely fabulous?!"

I knew my new companion had to be Cary.

I spun around to meet him. And he was, I could see, indeed a "flamer."

A real sweetheart. Effeminate in manner or not, he was a knockout of a male. I could not help but look him up and down.

His interest was in my eyes, not in my figure.

He shifted his glance from me to Jenna.

"Jenna," he enthused. "You've brought me a natural domina!"

"Do you really think she's a latent one?" Jenna responded.

"I can spot a natural dom or domina at fifty paces," he answered. "Are you going to introduce her or just stand there with your finger in your twat?"

"My finger's not in my twat, Cary, you foul mouthed pervert," Jenna answered with a laugh. "But let me introduce Colleen to you anyway. Zack just hired her as a swimming coach and counselor for the camp.

"Colleen, this gorgeous hunk of stuff is Cary."

Cary formally shook my hand.

"I see that you have a natural affinity for floggers," Cary began.

"Do you already have a little supply of torture instruments of your own?"

I told him I did not.

"You simply *must* get yourself armed, you know, Dear." he enthused. "Zack...ooo, that deliciously hung Zack. Zack will insist on it. I just know it. And he will be so peeved at me if I let you board the boat to Catalina without the means to beat the Hell out of the slaves who are Zack's and Alex's minions once you get there."

He went on for some time in that vein, talking as he took whips, paddles and canes out of the display cases and laid them out on a table over by the silhouettes and other targets.

He handed me a rattan cane from the batch of instruments he had laid on the table.

"Let me see how you inflict a smart spanking to Frank over there with this," he practically ordered me.

"Frank" was one of the free standing dummies. He had a prominent bare butt.

I gave a very satisfying set of blows to that butt with the cane.

The experience dampened my panties.

Maybe I really am a natural domina. That felt really good. Right down into my crotch.

Cary handed me one flogger after another. He and Jenna observed me as I tried them out, one by one.

For me, the beating of the dummies and the silhouettes was a true picnic. When the tip of the blacksnake and then the bullwhip flicked to the precise center of the targets, I received accolades from Jenna and Cary. A release such as I had never before experienced overcame me. I heard ooos and aahs. Twice I even received applause from them.

I knew I was performing before a truly savvy BDSM audience. And I felt proud of myself.

My physical coordination *is* excellent. I always knew that. So the wielding of the floggers simply came natural to me.

When Cary handed me the bullwhip to try out, I hit the bull's-eye on my chosen target.

"That was scrumptious, Darling," Cary commented. "But I was so hoping you could do better than that."

A bull's-eye is perfect. What did he expect?

"The beauty of the bullwhip is in the snap, Sweetie," he informed me. "When wielded correctly, the tip breaks the sound barrier as it stings its target. The snapping sound will make your sub flinch delightfully. And the speed with which the fucking cracker is sailing through the air makes it sting unlike any other whip.

"Most of these floggers, like the lovely cat-o'-nine-tails, leave nasty red slashes wherever they land. Just delightful. I just *love* welts, don't you? And they hurt like Hell. But the bullwhip doesn't leave a slash across the victim's raw skin. Instead, it leaves just one yummy imprint. And that sweet little sting is more painful on bare, exposed skin than anything on earth other than perhaps a bullet.

"I've only had one or two customers who can find the right wrist action to get one of these mothers to snap right.

"Give it another couple of tries and let's see if you can make Jenna and me jump off the floor at the sound of the fucking snap."

I knew what Cary was saying. I could feel within the core of my being what I would have to do to accelerate the knotted tip of that vicious thong so it would make its sound and inflict a very, very painful sting.

I gave it a try. The coordination of my shoulder, arm and wrist came together. I hit the target. But no resounding snap was generated.

I relaxed myself completely. As I do before taking a swan dive from the high board. Every muscle in my entire body fell into perfect balance.

Then, with the bullwhip firmly in my grasp, with the lethal fall resting comfortably on the floor, I swung the ten foot length off the ground to full extension over my head and behind my back. With an overhead throw and a violent flip of the wrist, the cracker hit a male silhouette squarely between the shoulders. The snap was as resounding as a fire cracker.

I cannot describe the satisfaction I felt from my accomplishment.

Jenna and Cary ran up and hugged me.

Cary removed his shirt, revealing a torso sculpted like Atlas himself.

He walked up to the wall, faced it, and grabbed onto two knobs that stretched his shoulders out as taut as they would extend.

"All right, Baby," he called back to me.

"Feet on the mark?"

"Yes," I assured him.

"Right onto my left shoulder blade. And with a snap!"

I thought that if I succeeded, the result might just yield me the happiest moment in my life.

I steadied myself, aligned my muscles, flipped that bull up into the air. And...

Crack!

Cary screamed with pain and fell to the floor in a heap.

Jenna and I ran up to him, alarmed.

Through his pouring tears he sobbed, "Colleen. You are the new Calamity Jane."

I guess that was a complement.

When Cary managed to get back up on his feet with our help and could speak again, he told me:

"I'll contact Zack. He'll wet his pants, he'll be so pleased. I'll tell him what supplies I'm recommending for you."

Jenna and I left the store while Cary was struggling to get his shirt back on.

I guessed I had impressed him.

As we were walking back to the bus stop, Jenna was gushing all over me.

I asked her what that crack was that Cary had made about a calamity

"Oh, yeah," she chuckled. "Calamity Jane. She's a historical figure. Part of our Wild West. She was famous for the way she could wield her bullwhip. One of her tricks was to knock the lit end off a cigarette held in her boyfriend's lips at ten feet.

"As a matter of fact, there are more women than men who are known for their prowess with the bull. And you know what, Colleen? I feel you'll join that group.

"Now let me tell you something. When you get to camp on Catalina, Zack and Alex will have spread the word about your mastery with the bull. And, I'm pretty sure that from Cary's recommendation to him, Zack's going to order a catsuit, boots, and a leather biker's cap for you. A full domina outfit. And any member of the staff who wants to can beg you to accept him or her as your slave."

Frankly, I could not comprehend what Jenna was even talking about. Catsuit? Boots? Slaves?

So I just smiled, nodded, and let what she was going on about flow into one ear and out the other.

There would be time enough to learn about this new world I had fallen into.

When we got back to our motel room we were both exhausted. We flopped into bed without so much as rubbing our palms all over each other's body.

That's how tired we were.

CHAPTER SEVEN

A Visitor

It was much later in the afternoon when the ringing of the telephone awakened us both.

Jenna dragged herself out of bed and went over to the desk to answer the damned thing.

"Yes, this is Jenna," she said.

"Zack?…Nice to hear your voice…Why certainly…Any time… We'll be expecting you then in about a half hour…Yeah, Colleen and I will be thrilled to death…Bye…"

"Guess who that was?" Jenna asked me when she'd hung up.

"I couldn't possibly guess," I joked. "From what I could hear from this end of your conversation, I gather our boss-man is coming calling on us."

We made ourselves up for his arrival and re-made the bed. Then, we just kind of sat on the edge of our seats until The Man knocked on the door.

I knew what to expect when he arrived. And was not surprised at what I saw.

Zachary Lund is what Jenna calls an alpha male. A dom for sure. His presence sends out pheneromes that cause your pussy to clench then dampen. Whatever the guy wanted, I was ready to submit to right there on the spot.

He greeted the two of us with a warm smile when he entered the room.

He kissed Jenna on the cheek then looked me up and down approvingly.

"Nice to have you aboard our enterprise, Colleen," he smiled.

"Alex tells me wonderful things about you. I know you'll be a credit to our camp program on Defoe Bay. The swimming and water sports program is very important in any summer camp. And at Camp Crusoe it is probably the main draw for most of our campers."

I could tell I was blushing at his warm welcome. And my knees were trembling from the appeal his presence was inflicting on my hormones.

"I had a call from Cary at the T4T shop not too long ago," the hunk of male went on. "He was raving about your ability in wielding the bullwhip."

More blushes. More weak knees.

"A girl with your looks who is a mistress of the bullwhip could be an enormously popular addition to our staff. Cary spotted you as a natural domina.

"So I just had to pop right over and check out your qualifications myself."

So! I guess it's showtime again.

"Alex has fully informed me about your BDSM credentials," Zack told me. "The spankings you submitted to from your father. The bondage, whipping and cock sucking from the Irish headmaster. The various floggings, humiliations and fellatio on board that ship. And, of course, the submissions you suffered from under Alex himself.

"But, I cannot help but wonder. Have you ever felt the kiss of the bullwhip yourself?"

I had to admit that I had never even seen a bullwhip until that very afternoon.

"Hmmm," Zack hummed. "Alex tells me you respond very favorably to spanking and flogging."

"Oh, yes, Sir," I answered with the expected enthusiasm. "I need punishment because I am quite inclined towards naughtiness and evil."

"Then," he said judiciously. "I assume you need disciplining periodically."

"Indeed I do, Master," I told him.

Zack marched over to the steamer trunk that sat by the western wall of the room.

He extracted a set of keys from his pocket, unlocked the trunk and lifted the lid.

I was very interested in standing up and gazing into that magic storage box. But I dared not do so. I think at some level I was afraid I might find out more than I yet wanted to know about what perversities dwelt within the soul of the man who had become not only my employer but the new-found master of my soul.

He removed a batch of lumber from that trunk. Yes, boards. Unpainted wooden boards. He ordered Jenna to go over to where he was, carry the assemblage to a spot in the middle of the room and assemble those pieces of lumber.

I could tell she knew exactly what to do because without hesitation she went to the lumber pile, gathered up the boards and planks, set them down on the specific spot mentioned by our boss and began to assemble some kind of artifact.

"Colleen," our master ordered me. "Go over and help Jenna put the spanking bench together. You will be expected to assemble it yourself henceforth."

Spanking bench! A tinker toy spanking bench! One wonder after another.

Jenna and I put the contraption together. It certainly was not complicated. It was actually nothing more than a kind of sawhorse. Four legs supporting a carpeted plank. If called upon to put one together myself at some time I knew I would encounter no difficulty whatsoever.

Zack then took three more objects out of his trunk.

"Colleen, here! Fetch these footcuffs and spreader bar while your little friend finishes her job."

I hastened over to him.

"Go over to one of those chairs and snap these cuffs around your ankles," he ordered gruffly.

Fetch? Foot cuffs? Spreader bar?

It was clear Jenna and I were in slave mode now. And the cuffs bode fair to prepare me for a bit of physical submission.

The cuffs were like short, wide leather fur-lined belts with D-rings attached. I encircled each of my ankles with one of the things and cinched them nice and tight the way I knew my master wanted me to.

"That's very nicely done, Colleen," Zack complimented me in a patronizing tone. "Now, would you be so kind as to stand over there facing the pretty bench? And don't forget to take your spreader bar with you."

I complied, of course.

The spreader bar was an extendable steel rod with clip hooks attached at the ends.

"Lay the spreader bar on the top plank," he ordered.

I did so.

"Press your lovely body up against the top of the bench now, won't you please, Honey?" he teased me.

"Isn't that carpeting on the top plank attractive," he asked.

"Yes, Sir," I answered. "Very attractive."

The carpeting had garish colors and an ugly paisley design on it. But I didn't feel like pointing that out to him.

"It's there for your comfort, Colleen. I *do* want you to feel comfortable," he joshed.

"Thank you, Sir," I responded as though he really had any desire for me to be comfortable while he did to me whatever he had in his sadistic mind.

"Now, spread your legs apart, Sweetie," he said in a most pleasant tone.

I did so.

"God damn it, Bitch," he yelled at me in a gruff tone that contrasted markedly from his speech up to that time. "I didn't tell you to mince your gams daintily apart. Spread 'em!"

Oh, dear!

So, I spread my legs quite wide apart.

"Grab the top of the bench, you stupid cow," he shouted.

I did so.

He stepped up behind me and gave my right leg a kick to the side that really smarted.

"More," he yelled. "Do I have to give you another God damned kick to get your fucking legs spread out wide enough?"

I complied, separating my feet so far apart that I thought I might just split right up the middle. I knew that if I hadn't been supporting myself sturdily on the top of the bench I would have toppled over.

"Right!" he said in a reasonable voice.

"Now, Jenna," he ordered. "Please retrieve the spreader bar from the bench and extend it so the fasteners can clip onto Colleen's cuffs. Screw in the holder nice and tight so the length doesn't slip.

Jenna was crouched down on the floor attaching me to that damned bar. The discomfort from the unnatural stretch was causing tears to run down my cheeks.

"Are you comfortable now, Kate?" Zack asked. "Or would you prefer that we extend that bar a bit farther?"

Farther? Is the man daft? Tell him it's just fine as it is.

"It's quite comfortable as it is, Master," I lied.

"That's just ducky, then, isn't it?" he teased.

"Now, lay your belly down onto the nice carpeted plank...very good...hold your hands up over your head...you know, as though you were about to dive into a pool. Now, lower your arms and head down towards the floor."

Jesus, Joseph and Mary! I was bent all the way over this contraption with blood rushing into my head.

"Just relax there, Dear," Zack intoned. "Get nice and comfy while I ask you a few questions.

"Are you legally in this country?"

"No, Sir," I responded.

"Then, I take it you are a God damned criminal," he accused.

It was very difficult to speak with my belly pressed against the plank and my upper body upside down. But I managed to grind out an answer.

"Yes, Master."

"Yes, Master, what?" he urged.

"Yes, Master. I am a God damned criminal."

"Why did you leave your native country and come sneaking over to America?" he asked.

I ground out an abbreviated version of the story about me and Jamie O'Doul. I knew Alex had already informed him of all that so I hoped the short version would suffice so he would let me get up from that torturous position.

"I'm shocked," the man claimed.

"You had sex with a student! A mere child! And you a teacher!

"You clearly need to be taught a lesson. We cannot have you compromising Camp Robinson Crusoe by molesting any of our campers, can we?"

I knew it would do no good to protest that I had already been punished again and again for the Jamie incident. So I simply agreed.

"Yes, Sir," I responded.

"'Yes, Sir' hardly seems an adequate answer, you Mick Slut," he raged.

The blood flushing my face and the difficulty breathing from my position was giving me a case of vertigo and a headache that was nearly insufferable. I had a hard time thinking. Yet I knew I needed to come up with a satisfactory response if I was to get this ordeal over with.

"I believe I need chastisement to help me remember not to do anything like that again," I managed to say.

It was the right response.

Obviously satisfied with what I had said, Zack lifted my short skirt up over my back and tore my panties as he ripped them down over my wide-spread legs.

That left me in as humiliatingly exposed condition as I'd ever been in my life before.

Bam!

His raw hand slapped down onto my exposed ass.

"You depraved wetback," he growled. "Take that on your worthless hide."

He administered one whack after another. He did not shift hands nor reverse from palm to knuckle side. The pain to his own palm did not appear to bother him in the least.

No one had ever absorbed all the pain when spanking me before. And, for some reason, that made me love the man as I'd never loved before.

He called me a worthless piece of shit, a degenerate, a pedophile, and worse and worse as the spanking continued nearly beyond my endurance level.

As a finishing touch, he slapped my exposed pussy so hard I felt I was going to expire.

The man was a genius spanker.

"Do you think you've learned your lesson, Bitch?" he inquired.

"Oh, yes, Master," I sobbed. "I am sure I've learned my lesson."

"Then get yourself out of that ridiculous position," he ordered. "I want to talk to you about some important matters.

"Jenna, detach her cuffs from the bar and set the bar on the floor."

Jesus! Just getting my legs back together was a chore of its own as I felt the click hooks snap off the bar.

I was more than anxious to get my head back up get away from that devilish bench.

It was a real struggle to do so, and I knew no one was going to help me.

But I slid my belly back and dropped to my knees on the floor. With an exertion of will I grabbed the top of the bench and pulled myself upright again.

And, as the blood drained out of my face and I found my equilibrium again I realized that I had just experienced the most erotic sensations I could remember.

When that bastard had given me that brutal slap on my cunt…I had come onto his fucking hand.

What an experience *that* had been.

Zack ordered me to pick up my ripped panties from the floor, remove my cuffs, and go sit in one of the chairs.

Ouch!

The wooden chair seat was far from comforting to my inflamed, painful, sorely beaten bottom.

I wiggled uncomfortably, which yielded no relief at all to the pain I was experiencing.

"Jenna," Zach said. "Why don't you pull your chair next to your little friend's? She looks like she could use company."

Jenna complied immediately, of course.

"Now, because you are good friends, I would like each of you to stick a finger up the other one's cunt while I address you."

My pussy was still smarting from that last wallop he'd given it, but because of the fact that it was still damp from my ordeal, the entry of Jenna's finger was softened somewhat.

As my index finger slid through her slit I was aware of how damp she was down there, too.

Jenna had been aroused by watching Zack spank me.

"Now, leave your fingers in each other while I talk to you," Zack instructed. "But no fluffing each other off. All right?"

I was acutely aware of what Zack was doing. Two young women, sitting next to each other with their fingers up each other's cunts while looking up at their dom and being told not to masturbate each other places them in a ridiculous, shameful, subservient situation.

I realized that what Jenna called BDSM is a practice that involves psychological bondage as much as physical.

Humiliation is as binding as ropes, cuffs or chains.

I tucked that bit of wisdom away in my mind for further use should I ever have a chance to become a domina myself.

My eyes followed Zack with some apprehension, wondering what to expect next, as he marched over to his trunk to rummage through and pick out some objects.

When he appeared back before us, it was with a mix of excitement and anxiety that I observed that the objects he had retrieved were a cat-o'-nine-tails and a bullwhip.

My red-welted cheeks informed me they were not ready to receive a flogging from either of those weapons.

As though lecturing to a class of dull-witted pupils he addressed us.

"In my left hand I hold a cat and in my right a bull.
'The function of a cat is to…"

He paused.

"Colleen," he interrupted himself.

I gave a startled jump at his calling my name.

"Yes, Sir?" I asked.

"You're not by any chance running your finger in and out of your friend's twat, are you?"

"No, Sir!" I answered smartly.

"Good," he continued. "I don't want your playful nature to distract your attention from what I am saying."

"Right, Master," I replied. "I'm all ears."

"Is your finger resting comfortably in your little friend's gash?" he inquired.

"Very comfortably, Sir," I answered, feeling the blush color my cheeks.

"Good," Zack said with a sigh.

"As I was saying, Colleen," he continued. "The function of the cat, the cat-o'-nine-tails, that is, is to inflict slash marks on the sub's epidermis. Red, angry, painful welts.

"Would you two care to see me demonstrate what I am saying?"

Jenna and I responded unhesitatingly in the affirmative.

"Fine," Zack said.

"Jenna, would you be kind enough to disrobe so I can accommodate your desire?"

"Yes, Master," my friend replied.

She stood up immediately and in a matter of less than a minute she was completely nude and her clothing was neatly folded on the chair she had just vacated.

"Be kind enough, Jenna, to step over to the Saint Andrew Cross, facing it."

She walked determinedly over to the western wall. "You know how to accommodate your body to the four points of the cross, Jenna," he said.

"Please assume the position."

She spread-eagled herself appropriately without a word or a whimper.

"Now, Colleen," he said, still in his professorial mode. "Kindly step up to the yellow mark on the floor. It is the right distance from which to administer a flogging. Flogging, you will recall, is a function of the cat.

He joined me at the mark.

"Now, would you please take this bullwhip from me so I can attend to the cat?

"Thank you.

"Both the cat and the bull profit by having their knotted ends soaked in vinegar. Since I do not happen to have any vinegar available at the moment, the pain on the miscreant at the cross will be relatively painless.

"Now, observe closely how I handle the flogger."

Without further warning he swung the strands across his body to the left, then unfurled the thongs with a sickening whish across Jenna's bare back.

Pow!

Since she was not bound to the cross, the blow knocked her down to the ground.

"Please re-assume the position, Jenna dear," Zack coaxed. "I want our new camp counselor to see first-hand the signature left by a cat-o'-nine-tails."

Jenna struggled back up and spread her limbs back into the position, sobbing up a storm.

"Note the beautiful patterns left by the instrument, Colleen," he told me. "A series of welts, and some lovely bloody trails.

"Do you suppose you can fling the strands across your friend's lovely back making a criss-cross pattern?"

I was not proud of what I felt at that moment. The thought of inflicting a torturous set of criss-cross streaks on Jenna's red-welted back shot a jolt of adrenaline into my very libido. I felt a craving to inflict as much pain as my master had on my girlfriend.

I received the cat from my dom. I toed the yellow mark. I relaxed, then focused the muscles in my back, my abdomen, my arms and my wrists into the enterprise.

Zing!

Jenna sank to the floor howling with pain as the strands I had flung bit into her tender skin.

"Do stand up, Jenna darling," Zack ordered. "We want to see the pattern your playmate has made on your soft skin."

Jenna struggled up, body wracked with pain as demonstrated by her copious tears and sobs.

"Now *do* take the position again, Love," Zack told her. "So we can take a look at Colleen's work."

The welts I had inflicted were neither as deep nor as red as the ones left from Zack's flogging. But, they weren't too bad either.

I awaited Zack's verdict.

"Not bad, Girl," he affirmed my own appraisal. "Needs work. Lots of work. Practice, practice, practice.

"You seem to have real potential."

Do you know what I felt as I saw my friend still shuddering from the pain I had visited upon her?

Pride.

"Now, Girls," Zack said evenly. "Go back and sit in your chairs again. I have a few more points to make.

"And, oh, yes. This time put your own finger into your own koozie. But do not play with yourself while your finger itches to bring you off. I want your undivided attention."

As Jenna and I dutifully returned to our chairs and inserted our fingers in our twats, Zack put the cat-o'-nine-tails back in his trunk.

I hoped that meant that he wasn't planning on flogging me with it.

He returned to stand before us now with only the bullwhip in his hand.

"Now, Colleen dear," he began. "Most whips, cudgels and paddles can be used by virtually any dom or domina to impose pain, chastisement, subjection and humiliation. But only one master or mistress in a hundred can deliver the choicest of scourges – the bullwhip.

"You, Love, may just have the coordination the subtlety…the gift… of being able to crack the bull anywhere on your victim's…or should I say, your subject's… nerve infested body.

"You cannot imagine how pleased I would be to discover that you possess the knack.

"That is to say, you may have been blessed with an inherent gift to be a very top top, a mistress of the purple art, a true dominatrix.

"But, if you are to be a star at our camp on the island, which is certainly a possibility, you must know how the bull's kiss elicits raptures in your very soul."

And here I thought I had been hired to teach children to swim and engage in water sports. Better not bring that up at the present.

"Since your panties are already rent and are history, you should be able to slip into your birthday suit in a trice," he said with a flicker of a smile.

Birthday suit? Buck arse naked he means.

I took my finger out of my gash, slipped out of my clothes and felt my nipples pop out to point themselves in this very male male's direction.

The fur-lined footcuffs were still over by the spanking bench.

"Go fetch the footcuffs by the bench, Girl," Zack ordered.

Fetch again. And "Girl."

I hustled over to the bench and retrieved the damned things.

"Now, sit on the floor there and put those cuffs on again, nice and tight, while Jenna hastens over to the trunk to find you a matching pair of handcuffs," he directed.

As I sat uncomfortably on the floor on my still very sensitive, pained bottom re-fastening the cuffs, Jenna did as she was told and brought the handcuffs over to me.

I had my footcuffs snuggly attached to my ankles and Jenna cinched the handcuffs on my wrists.

By the smile on her face it was clear to me that she was joyfully anticipating my getting delightfully tortured by our dom as she had been.

"Get your God damned ass over to the cross, Slut," my master addressed me.

From "Dear" to "Slut," now. Painful experience ahead for sure.

I did not have to be told what to do. As Zack extended the cross-bars of the cross to uncomfortable widths, I faced the contraption and spread my arms and legs to the attachment rings.

Snap, snap, snap, snap!

Zack had me attached and practically bisected in painful bondage.

As he stepped back to the mark, his boots beat the floor with hard, distinct tattoos.

"Prepare yourself, you Irish cunt," he bellowed. "This is the kiss the bull delivers when properly administered."

I heard the snap just a micro-second before I felt the sting on my left butt-cheek.

Jesus! I did not believe the human body could endure such a sharp pain and survive.

I yelped, lost control of my muscles and would have slumped down onto the floor if I had not been so tightly bound. And, I was in too much pain to be embarrassed that my bladder had emptied a flood of pee onto the floor beneath me.

When I heard the next sharp crack of the whip, my expired muscles spasmed into a violent clenching action. In that split second my panicked body did not know where the burning sting would land.

God Almighty! On my right cheek.

My yelp must have resounded blocks away. I had never experienced such divine agony.

I thought my whole ass must be on fire.

My bowels emptied on the floor in a stinking mess.

Subjection! Agony! Humiliation!

The vision of the exaltation I had felt when I had landed my thunderous whack with the bullwhip on Cary's shoulder blade flashed into my mind.

Power! Pain! Rapture!

I knew that these were mine at either end of the sacred bullwhip.

"You love it, don't you, Bitch!?" Zack exulted.

"Maybe you don't think you can bear any more. Well, you *will* bear more. As much more as I choose to bless you with. Hang there for a while above that mess of shit and piss you've squandered on the floor beneath you…"

I knew the bastard had at least one more blow to deliver. I wanted it right then to get it over with. I wanted him to delay it because I could not stand another blow. In short, I did not know *what* I wanted.

Crack!

Yikes!

Right in the middle of my back.

I had heard the expression "wracked with pain." I had not truly understood it before.

I was so convulsed with sobs and so blinded with tears that I was transported to another world.

A world in which I orgasmed and my jism added to the offal I had deposited on the floor beneath me.

"Do you think you can remember how that feels?" Zack was saying to me.

I could just barely eke out my affirmative answer.

How could I ever possibly forget the agony and the ecstasy?

"Good girl," Zack said in the same tone he would use to say "good dog."

"Jenna," he said to my girlfriend. "I would like you to amble over there and unclip the filthy Irish slut from her bonds. Once you've undone the clip hooks, let her uncinch her own cuffs. She's a big enough girl to take care of that."

When Jenna released me from my bondage, I slumped onto the floor right into my own offal that I had released in my anguish and my euphoria.

Zack came over and stood above my prostrate form.

'Colleen!" he said. "You are a stinking mess down there. Jenna and I cannot bear the sight or smell of you.

"So we are going to walk over to the Abbey Coffeehouse on North Robertson. While we're gone, do manage to get yourself cleaned up and decent looking. And before we get back, you had better get that putrid mess you're lying in tidied up and get the stench out of this room. It smells like an Irish whorehouse in here.

"And, I know you are aware that there will be unpleasant consequences for you if you and this room are not in acceptable condition when we return.

"Come, Jenna. Leave the slut to clean up her wretched mess."

And with that benediction Zack and Jenna marched out of the room leaving me still retching and in tears.

When they left, I sat in the mess I had made and managed to uncinch my cuffs.

I could not manage to stand at first and began to crawl towards the bathroom, leaving a trail of muck in my wake.

By the time I got to the bathroom door I managed to get my aching body up off the floor so I could at least walk to the shower.

When I turned on the shower, the water was both welcome and painful on my ravaged skin.

I awkwardly managed to soap myself and rid my body of the grunge.

Bit by bit I was able to dry myself off and navigate back into the livingroom.

Then, fairly stable, and clothed and in a presentable condition, I walked to the motel office.

When I entered I was greeted by a young man rather than the girl who had been there before.

I told him I was a guest in Room Seven.

I wondered if he had heard my recent screams of agony. If so, he gave no indication.

I told him we had an accident in the room and that I needed to tidy it up a bit.

"I'm afraid the maids are not on duty at this hour," he told me. "But I can let you into their storage closet."

That was fine with me.

So, with cleaning supplies I got my mess mopped up and disposed of.

There was air freshener among the supplies which I sprayed around.

I then aired out the room.

And when Zack and Jenna came merrily back into the room about a half-hour later it was in condition to welcome them.

Zack had returned in professorial mode rather than that of arrogant, despotic dom.

He allowed Jenna and me to sit with ladylike formality, our hands folded primly in our laps, as he lectured to me from above.

"Colleen," he enunciated crisply. "I have *so* enjoyed meeting you. I believe you have the makings of a potentially valuable member of our staff.

"When you get to our camp on Catalina, you will not only be my employee. You will be my slave. As are all our staff members.

"Of course Alex will also share in your mastery.

"But Camp Robinson Crusoe is not a despotism. We are quite democratic in many ways. You may choose to ask any member of the staff from the dishwasher to the crafts counselor (Jenna, I knew) to be your dom or domina.

"And likewise, you may accept any member of the staff who requests it of you to be your slave.

"But, should you accept a person as slave, it is your responsibility to discipline him or her as strictly as Alex and I will discipline you."

What a revelation that was to me.

It was difficult at the time for me to imagine that anyone, for any reason, might choose to submit himself or herself to me. But, should that occur, I knew I would be able to be as cruel, as demanding, as merciless, and as punishing as I knew Zackary Lund and Alex Allen could be.

The new goal I just established for myself was not to become a domina. But to become something more pleasure giving yet.

I vowed to become *Colleen the Dominatrix.*

Zack told Jenna to take me back to T4T the next morning.

"I will have informed Cary exactly what to assemble for Colleen," he told Jenna.

"I am purchasing a lovely assortment of flogging and spanking products for her. Including, of course a ten foot tapered six-plait rawhide bullwhip with a leather popper with a rotating handle."

Still speaking to Jenna about what he was buying for me, Zack continued:

"I am also ordering a spandex catsuit, a pair of high-heeled, thigh-length boots and a leather biker's cap for her. The outfit will be delivered to me and I will present it to Colleen when and if I judge her to have passed from domina to dominatrix sometime in the future. She will have to prove herself worthy of the uniform, of course.

"Among the items Cary will include in Colleen's kit will be a nine-inch by three-inch dildo, an extra large ring gag and a black blindfold.

"We leave for Catalina eight days from now. On the morning of our departure either Alex or I, or perhaps both of us, will test our Colleen's adeptness at deep-throat.

"Colleen will be blindfolded and wearing the ring gag that morning, which will allow entry of Alex's seven by two inch cock or my nine by three into her throat while any tell-tale sounds on her part will be muffled.

"If her throat is not compatible with the organ of either of her masters, not only will she be severely punished. You will be as well.

"So train your little friend well, Jenna."

And without so much as a "good-bye" he opened the door and strode out.

Once the door closed behind our master, Jenna and I fell into each others arms and kissed each other deeply as we groped all over each other.

Jenna's hands on my flayed and spanked skin drew delightful shudders of pain throughout my abused body. I loved it.

And I purposely rubbed my hands roughly over the welts I had raised on her body and was rewarded by the frissons of pain and pleasure that radiated back to me from her tingles.

"Can you teach me to accommodate our masters' massive dongs in my tiny throat within the week?" I whispered in her ear.

"Trust me," she answered. "I'll get you trained and ready if it kills me."

I loved the viciousness implied in her answer.

"Are you pissed at me for flogging you at the cross?" I asked, pretty sure of the kind of answer I would get.

Jenna pulled herself even closer into me, so we stood pussy to pussy with our arms clutching us into intimate, suggestive contact.

We exchanged deep glances, separated our bodies and hand in hand we headed for the bed.

On the way to bed, I noticed that Zack had not put the two pairs of cuffs and the spreader bar back into his trunk. They were neatly arranged on top of the spanking bench.

How thoughtful!

"I wonder how come our boss forgot to tuck these little items back into his trunk," I mentioned.

"No doubt they are meant for his two minions to use," Jenna smiled. "Toys for the two of us to play with.

I'm sure we'll find a use for them tomorrow."

"I certainly hope so," I replied.

With that thought in mind, we hopped into bed for a bit of unbound fun before going to sleep

The mutual masturbation, the sixty-nine and the extensive body lickings we gave each other's welts and clits expressed the unspoken understanding we had of each other.

CHAPTER EIGHT

The Learning Curve

Starting the morning after Zack's visit, the first thing Jenna and I did before even going out for breakfast was deep-throat training.

Zack had given us a deadline. He told us we would leave for Catalina in eight days. And that on the morning before sailing off, my adeptness at the practice would be tested. And that if I failed to pass, Jenna and I would both be "severely punished."

He had gratuitously given us the dimensions of both his and Alex's members. And he told us Cary would have a giant size dildo, an extra large ring gag and a blindfold for me in preparation for the great event.

It was clear that if I could learn to accommodate the dildo and the gag while wearing the hoodwink, I should be able to pass the test when the fateful day arrived.

Jenna had three sizes of O gags in her supplies, a one-and-a-quarter inch, a one-and-a-half inch and a two inch.

We would begin with the smallest O gag and the smallest dildo and work me up to the super-sized products Cary was holding for me.

On that first morning, Jenna bound the smallest of her O gags into my mouth and inserted her smallest dildo through it.

On those trials, I sputtered, drooled and gagged as soon as the ersatz prick got past my teeth.

Jenna told me that was a normal enough reaction. That the procedure took some getting used to. And that by the time we left for the island I would have learned not only to accommodate a man-sized prick into my throat. But that I would *love* it.

We'd see.

After a half-hour of blowing that pint-sized dick, I gave it a try blindfolded.

Not bad!

I knew I'd pleasure Zack, Alex, or both with flying colors before boarding the boat for Catalina. For I would practice, practice, practice.

When she'd removed the dildo from my mouth through the O gag for the last time, she took my blindfold off and uncinched the gag.

As I looked up at her, she bent down and kissed me deeply. So cunt-clenchingly deeply.

"Breakfast time," she announced cheerfully.

We went to The Abbey for a light breakfast and returned to our room for a bit of sport before heading off to T4T to see Cary and pick up the new toys Zack had purchased for me.

Before we'd gone off to The Abbey, Jenna had lavished me with that panty-drenching kiss.

When we got back to the room after breakfast, I believed it was my turn to take the lead and be the top.

I faced up to her, wrapped my arms around her lithe body, grasping her firmly by the ass, and pulled her to me pussy to pussy.

I then licked her lips until they opened and I explored her gums with my tongue until she slipped her own tongue under mine.

With my hands tight against her ass I swayed her hips from side to side so that her mound grazed my own lasciviously.

She firmly grabbed my ass and maneuvered my own hips so we were in a mutual grind against each other, cunt sliding back and forth against cunt.

Without a word to each other, we broke away from our kiss-grind to get out of our clothes.

As soon as we were nude, we made for the bed.

We stretched out on the bed, lying on our sides facing each other.

I saw that her nipples had protruded and knew quite well that mine did too.

We each seemed to know instinctively that it was time for a bit of nipple play.

I licked a finger and ran it in circles around her aureoles. She took the hint and grazed my own, avoiding my nipple tips completely.

The finger-play on each other's pebbled aureoles had the effect of forcing blood into our nipples, elongating them farther still.

Her nipples hardened into blood red knobs just begging my lips to circle each one and suck it into an obscene protrusion.

And, as hard as those luscious tips entreated, my own tits were demanding identical relief.

Jenna made the first move and dove her warm moist mouth onto my left boob.

I sighed a deep sigh and whispered "Thank you, Luv" as I lay over onto my back to watch her in the mirror above as she serviced my extreme mammary need.

I could feel the dampness that was forming at my crotch. And thanks to the mirror above, I could actually see my cunt glisten with the welcome moisture.

What a turn-on.

She had me fully aroused as she leaned farther across my chest to give equal treatment to my other yearning nipple.

She bit down gingerly on that nipple and then rapidly switched to the other with an equally brisk bite.

God! I nearly came on the spot.

I reached a hand down towards her snatch to offer some kind of reciprocation when she sat straight up in bed, abandoning my happy titties.

"Time out!" she shouted, forming her lovely hands into a T.

Time out?! Now?!! Is she barmy?

Leaving me totally amazed and horny, Jenna leaped out of bed and hustled over to the spanking bench.

She retrieved the four cuffs Zack had left for us. I began to get a feel for how the wind was blowing.

She then marched deliberately over to the chest of drawers. From the bottom drawer, where I had surmised she kept her toys, she took out that petite dildo I'd been practicing on before breakfast and the lengths of rope she had previously bound me with.

The course she was pursuing grew clearer in my mind with every object she collected.

The next piece of equipment she took out of her treasure trove was an object I had never seen before and could not figure out at all.

Well, everything in due time, I always say.

I had been sitting up in bed, quietly running a happy finger up and down my slit with one hand and roughly squeezing my aroused nipples with the other while watching my girlfriend's shenanigans.

She returned to the bedside, placed the mysterious object whose function I still could not fathom and the pint-sized dildo on the nightstand.

"Here," she ordered me, handing me the footcuffs. "Put these around your ankles nice and tight."

As I followed her command I knew that I had just willingly given up my earlier resolve to be the top in the coming escapades.

I had little doubt that I was about to learn a few maneuvers that would stand me in good stead when and if I graduated to the position of butch domina.

When I had the footcuffs tightly in place I held out my arms to her in token of surrender to whatever she had in mind.

Jenna strapped the cuffs onto my wrists and had me lie down spread-eagle in the center of the large bed.

I had a good idea what would happen next.

With two of the rope strands she attached the D-rings of my handcuffs to eyebolts at the headboard to hold my upper body firmly down onto the mattress below.

I was familiar enough with the sensations inherent in having my arms spread out in bondage.

Her next action was quite a surprise.

She attached my legs to the posts at the foot of the bed. But she brought the ropes up to eyebolts halfway up the post and, with hearty yanks, pulled on the strands until my ass was just barely touching the mattress.

I was trussed up somewhat like a lopsided hammock above the bed, with my legs stretched out so far my pussy lips were splayed out.

Staring up at my reflection in the ceiling mirror I was entranced by seeing my glistening, gaping pussy. It reflected my stirrings at that moment.

That cunt of mine was fairly screaming to be played with.

When I looked away from the satisfying reflection I gazed at Jenna who now had the junior-sized dildo in her hand.

Engaging her eyes with mine she inserted that little sucker into her mouth and began running it lewdly back and forth as though giving great head to a little cock.

It was enough to make me wet my nether parts.

And, as a matter of fact, that was exactly what was happening to me. My gash was getting soaked and wetting the sheets beneath me.

Jenna took that spit-slicked dildo out of her mouth and traced it about my lips. I extended my tongue to give the little sweetie a few licks of my own, but Jenna kept it hovering just barely out of reach. How frustrating! In a naughty but nice way.

She finally relented, letting me lick the shaft from balls to piss-hole. I loved it.

She then let the bulb rest on my lips so I could suck the fake cock down into my desperate mouth and wrap my lips around the darling little number.

"Get it as spit-drenched as you can, Babe," Jenna told me. "Your cunt is getting nice and wet, but this dildo will feel even better down there slathered with your spit and mine."

The mirror above my head reflected an additional action going on next to me. Jenna was playing with her own mound, running a finger up and down her slit, giving little love slaps to her clit, and, all in all, just having herself a time while regaling me with the dildo.

When she chose to remove the slippery darling from my mouth and carry it down to my gaping hole, my pussy fairly whispered "Thank you."

She traced circles around my pussy lips with the head of the dildo. Then she ran it up and down the length of my snatch.

Ooo! I could take *that* all day long.

Then, when she inserted the dildo into my channel, I was fascinated watching in the mirror as I was being fucked royally.

When Jenna held the penetrating object still, by bending and unbending my knees I could thrust my butt up and down, humping myself merrily along, working that pecker at my own speed and thrust.

And, occasionally, I even managed to direct the sweet little member right over my g-spot.

God! Was that ever wonderful!

I could feel massive pre-orgasmic shudders crescendoing throughout my body. I could hardly wait to see myself come as I stared intently at the mirror above.

I'm right on the verge. I'm ready. I'm ready!

When "Pow."

My girlfriend literally pulled the plug on me.

"Oh, no, you little slut," she admonished. "You're going to have to learn to give up instant gratification. Because, Bitch. You are not going to come until I let you come. Get it?"

"Yes, Mistress," I agreed. But oh so reluctantly. I really was desperate to get my rocks off.

I knew Jenna had to have some other trick up her sleeve. Well, she was buck-ass naked, so there was no sleeve involved. What was involved was some new wicked treat or humiliation for her to lay on me.

It made no difference whether it would be humiliation or a sensory thrill. I was more than ready for her to bring it on,

With a puckish smile my mistress reached over to the bedside stand and picked up the object that posed such a mystery to me.

What is *that thing?*

"So," she gloated. "I suppose you think you're the only one around here privileged to wear a gag. Don't you, you selfish self-indulgent harpy? Do I have news for you, you drab floozy!

"This time I wear the gag. And at the same time, I get to suck cock at *my* tempo. And guess what? While I'm mouthing and sucking and licking to my own pleasured beat, you are going to get fucked.

"What do you think of that?"

"O.K. with me, Mistress," I replied.

She slapped me a hard on right across my face.

Ow. That stings…But good!'

"Didn't your mother teach you good manners? You Irish are barely civilized. What are you suppose to say?"

She held her open hand above my face ready to smack me another good one if I didn't give her the right answer.

"Thank you, Mistress," I enunciated very clearly. "Thank you very much!"

"That's more like it, Tramp," she responded, removing her hand from above my face. "You must always thank me when I go out of my way to teach you, discipline you, slap you silly, or even deign to abide you in my presence.

"I want you to take a good look at this delightfully designed double-dildo penis gag now."

She held the plastic entity above my upward gaze and explained its function to me.

As she showed me the construction of the gag she demonstrated its functions.

It was, indeed, a gag. But quite unlike the O gag that holds the mouth open to allow the entrance of a penis into the recipient's oral cavity.

This gag was composed of two dildos pointing in opposite directions.

The smaller dildo, as Jenna explained to me, is two inches long with a two inch diameter. The bulb at the end was rosy pink with flared lips and a pretty little pee-hole at the very tip. Who could imagine a function for such a small dick? It made the dildo Jenna had been inserting down towards my tonsils in the morning seem a colossus.

The dildo extending in the other direction was seven inches long and the same diameter as its counterpart.

"Now, just so you can get a feel for how this marvelous toy feels to the domina, I am going to put this darling implement in your fucking mouth. The short-dick side, that is."

I gaped, and as I did so Jenna unceremoniously shoved the tiny dildo into my yap.

When I looked up at myself in the mirror, I perceived the unlikely vision of a seven inch long hard dong emerging from my mouth.

Jenna removed the device with a flourish and gazed at me expectantly.

Why was she looking at me like that?

Smack! Right across the kisser.

Oh, yes. I remembered.

"Thank you, Mistress," I said quickly enough so as not to receive a second resounding slap.

"Manners, manners, Tart," Jenna said. "You mustn't forget to say 'thank you.'"

"Thank you for reminding me," I hastened to say.

Jenna grabbed the bottle of lube that was a fixture on our nightstand and gave a healthy slathering to the seven inch protrusion of the gag.

"Now, you good-for-nothing shithead" she cooed. "Get ready for a fucking you'll never forget."

She strapped the gag into her mouth, burrowed down into my cunt and rammed the business end of the object right up into my old koozie.

Yikes! Ooo!

"Thank you, Mistress!"

The reflection I saw in the mirror was weirdness itself. It looked like Jenna was fucking me with her face while strumming her own snatch. You know, it looked like what she'd previously called "muff diving".

Of course, in a sense, muff diving *was* what she was doing.

But in another sense what she was actually doing, I realized, was sucking, tonguing and slobbering luxuriously on the bulb of a two-inch round imitation cock. She was taking her own sweet time enjoying the feeling a horny butch gets giving mouth music at a beat and rhythm that matches her own sensual needs without regard to anyone else.

Thus, the fucking I was getting from the other side of the gag was way too slow and lethargic to ever get me to a full orgasm.

So, although I have to admit that I enjoyed the screwing I was getting, I knew I would never get off from it.

Jenna was having herself a time with her salacious sucking while keeping me dangling in libidinal limbo.

What an exotic, infernal torture! It drove me crazy. I loved it.

She finally withdrew the dildo from my cunt and took off the gag.

"All right, Girl," she announced. "I'm just on the verge of coming. So I'm going to release you from your restraints and let you fluff yourself off to a grand orgasm at your own private pace."

So, as I watched my girlfriend in the ceiling mirror getting herself off to a wild, juicy orgasm, I had a full view of my own cunt as I was driving three of my fingers into my hole with one hand and stroking my clit with the other.

The two of us were howling, laughing and crying in a libidinous duet with our legs curled around each other as we came in orgasm after orgasm after orgasm.

My God. Life was *good*!

Relaxed and satisfied after my bondage experience that culminated in getting my rocks off in a blaze of glory, I assumed that Jenna was through with me and that it would be my turn to tie her up and have my way with her.

Wrong!

We sat up in bed and kissed each other deeply.

I began to uncinch my cuffs when Jenna gave me a wallop on the head.

Ouch! What the Hell?

"Who the fuck told you you could take off the cuffs, Douche Bag?" she thundered. "I'm not through with you yet."

"It's time for some trapeze work."

"Trapeze work?" I questioned.

"Haven't you ever gone to the circus, Mick?" she queried. "Or don't they have such things in that benighted country you sneaked so shamelessly out of?"

I could see she had her right hand poised to slap me a good one if I did not answer promptly.

"Oh, yes, Mistress," I hurriedly replied. "We have circuses back home."

I thought a look of disappointment crossed her visage when she lost an opportunity to knock me silly again for not replying fast enough.

"Look up at the ceiling, Dumbass!" she commanded. "No, not at the goddam mirror where you've been salaciously entranced by gazing at your own fucking cunt. Look around at the other parts of the ceiling."

I took in the ceiling with a wide-ranged glance.

"What do you see?" she asked.

"Pulleys," I answered. "Lots of pulleys, Mistress."

"Very good," Jenna sneered. "Pulleys. What sorts of things are dangling from the ropes strung through those pulleys?"

"Hooks, Domina. And bars and straps and I don't know what all."

"Get your dimpled ass out of bed and go find the pulley that's holding a trapeze bar."

That was easy. There was a bar suspended from a pulley that was at a far end of the room. I hurried over and pointed to it.

"Here is a trapeze, Mistress," I called to her.

"All right, Slut," Jena called back to me. "Kneel down directly underneath it and hold your hands up high over your shiteating head."

I complied as I watched my domina go over to the dresser, rummage though her toys and bring out a dildo belt and a blindfold.

She strapped on the belt, grabbed the lube tube from the nightstand and ambled over with the lumbering gate of a real bulldyke to where I was kneeling.

She released the end of the rope that led to its pulley from its mooring and lowered the trapeze to the level of my upraised hands.

"Grab the trapeze nice and tight," my domina ordered. "Keep your legs folded back and when you have a firm purchase on the trapeze you'll find yourself hanging nicely there with your knees a couple of inches above the floor."

When I was hanging on the bar as directed, Jenna spoke to me rather harshly.

"Stay hanging there while I go over to the dresser to get some clip hooks, the spreader bar, and a rattan cane to entertain you with. You'll love the next party

"And remember, when I'm through with you it will be your turn to play top and mine to be your bottom."

The reversal of roles sounded good to me. But, I have to admit, the chance to experience some additional pain and humiliation made my crotch dampen. When she returned from her trip to her treasures in the bottom drawer of the dresser she was carrying the items she had described to me.

She laid everything but two clip hooks on the floor and lowered the trapeze bar by a few inches.

"Now spread your hands out to the two extreme ends of the bar, Piss Pot," she ordered. "I need to get you really hanging like the rotten bag of crap you truly are."

I extended my arms as commanded, and, click/click, my cuffs were fastened to rings that were welded to each end of the trapeze.

"Upsy-daisy," Jenna called out. "Stand up as I pull on this rope."

I did my best to scramble up as she tugged on her end of the rope.

When I was standing with my arms extended to their fullest she ordered me to spread my legs as wide as I could.

I no sooner was spread out than she moved the damned spreader bar between my feet and clamped my footcuffs to the ends.

Talk about "spread eagle." I felt more like a spread out turkey.

There I was, hanging from the trapeze, my legs spread out to their maximum, my pussy lips pulling apart, and completely vulnerable to Jenna's sadistic whimsies.

"Mmm," my top hummed. "What lovely meat I have here to devour at will. I think I'll sample some neck."

She bit gently into my neck at the jugular. Jesus! I couldn't inch away from the shivery sensation.

She ran her tongue up to that sensitive spot just behind my earlobe and traced circles there. The currents shot from that point straight down to my gash and sent waves of moisture down my thighs as she nibbled on my earlobe.

To even things up she attacked my neck on the other side and followed up with a repeat performance.

The effect was to make me quite juicy down below.

She then began to lick me very slowly and deliberately under my chin. Then, grabbing my ass with her two hands she slobbered a trail of spit down between my boobs and kept going until her tongue was swirling about in my bellybutton.

Somewhere within my body electric sparks were whirling around.

She separated my ass cheeks gently and rubbed my asshole as her lips descended to my awaiting open cleft.

I was squirming and moaning, attempting to press my quim against her tongue. I desperately wanted to swallow that tongue with my hole. But all I could do was hang there and pant as she persisted in just licking the labia.

This was way too much cunt teasing. All I really wanted now was to come. I would go bonkers if she tried to keep me there on the edge.

"Fuck me, Jenna," I pleaded. "Please. For mercy's sake. Fuck me!"

"Shit eating Cunt," Jenna shrieked.

"How *dare* you order *me*! You need to learn who's the boss dyke around here.

"I'm going to teach you a lesson you will never forget!"

The girl *did* sound authoritative.

And I knew I'd cooked my goose as far as getting any chance of shooting off my rocks for the moment.

She picked up the damned blindfold, slipped behind me and pulled it down over my head.

Everything went dark. The hoodwink cut out every bit of light in the room. My feeling of vulnerability increased many-fold.

"Apologize to me, Wench," she screamed as a wild stinging pain insulted my midriff.

I realized that she had picked up the rattan cane and had administered a sharp whack to my belly.

Man! Out of the blue, or out of the darkness to be precise, that was an unkind cut. And it hurt like Hell.

"I'm sorry," I pleaded through my tears.

"Not sufficient," Jenna responded with a caning across my tits.

No! Not on my tender tits!

"I'm sorry, Mistress," I attempted.

The next blow was across my delicate thighs.

I never really knew until then how very tender the flesh is high up on the thigh. I was consumed with sobs.

"Where are your manners, Whore?" was Jenna's next hint of what kind of answer she expected.

Jenna stopped talking and proceeded to inflict a series of blows to my thighs, belly, and tits. I tried to cry out to make her stop, but my words simply fell upon the dark silence that enveloped me.

There was a pause in the caning. I hoped that meant the end of the torture. A torture that had convulsed me into a pre-orgasmic seizure.

Then came the cruelest blow of all, up between my thighs and onto my perineum, that tender spot halfway between my cunt and my asshole.

Blindfolded, I hadn't been able to see it coming. Which somehow increased the agony.

"Thank you, Mistress!" I screamed. "Thank you very much, Domina!"

My tears were soaking my blindfold. I was shaking with sobs. My whole body was a hanging mass of pain.

"You took too long to remember your manners, Shitface," Jenna informed me. "So your sweet little ass is about to get the tanning it deserves. What would you say to ten blows?"

"That would be very nice, Mistress," I lied. "Thank you for suggesting it."

"You bet it will be nice, you cunt teaser. You count out the blows as I administer them. And be sure to thank me nicely after each one."

That girl really laid her cane onto my poor suffering butt. Lord! How each stroke stung.

As directed, I counted as each blow whacked onto my pathetically abused ass. And my expressions of thanks somehow got delivered amidst my cries, sobs, shrieks and curses.

I counted my last.

"TEN! Thank you, Mistress."

I was hanging limply from the trapeze bar, my shoulder muscles a mass of pain augmenting the grueling tingle from the welts on my poor backsides.

I was ready to be released.

Not released from the bondage, mind you.

Released from the pent-up passion that the ruthless beating had engendered in my pussy.

I desperately needed to come!

Jenna removed my blindfold. The sudden intrusion of light into my eyes added an additional element of discomfort to the pain that radiated from my ass and the passion that throbbed in my snatch.

Jenna was standing in front of me wearing nothing but her dildo strap with the medium-sized dildo pointing coyly toward me.

She seemed to be masturbating the realistic cock. Why? To tease me?

No, I realized. What she was doing was lubricating it well from the lube tube.

Oh, thank heavens! It looked like she was going to fuck me. To give me the release I so ardently sought. She was going to be kind, considerate and loving. My dear, thoughtful Jenna.

Wrong!

She squirted a large gob of the goop onto her hands and stepped behind me.

Behind?

Next thing I knew she was rubbing the lube all over my asshole.

Then one of her lubed fingers shot up through the hole into my ass.

Ooo!

Out came the finger, and two fingers replaced it, thrusting into me in its place.

Eek!

Out came the two fingers. What a relief.

But when they were followed by three of her fingers I gave a cry that must have been audible up on Melrose Avenue.

"Now, Baby," Jenna snarled at me. "As a nice finishing touch to the entertainment I've provided for you, you are going to get cornholed."

Cornhole? I was somewhat aware of the American word. It's what's called "buggery" back home in Ireland. I was looking for a good fucking up the kooze, not into the bunghole.

But did I have a choice?

Rhetorical question.

I felt the tip of Jenna's dildo touch my puckered rosebud. Oh-oh.

When she thrust that thing into me, her body slammed against my welt-infested ass.

"Ouch! That hurts!" I complained.

"Shut up, Whiner," Jenna grumbled, giving me a more intense bump than before.

"One more word of complaint and I'll stop pleasing your rosy ass and go back to applying the cane another ten times."

I knew that was more of a promise than a threat. So I said no more and made no sounds other than a continuous series of whimpers.

When she had had her way with me, and I had really grown to love the sensations of being fucked up the ass while my cheeks became more and more inflamed by the contact with Jenna's pubis, she released me from the trapeze and the spreader bar.

I would have crumpled to the floor. But she caught me and supported me as she led me to the bed.

I fell into the bed head first. I needed to leave my fanny cooling in the refreshing air.

Jenna lovingly removed my four cuffs and expertly put them on herself.

"Turn over, Kid," she told me. "Your ass can take the pressure of the soft sheets.

"What you need now is a sweet orgasm or two. And you're going to get a honey as a reward for the pleasure you gave me in doing you so satisfyingly."

I turned over (ouch!), spread my knees (ooo!) and yielded myself to ministrations of Jenna's educated tongue, lips and mouth to my most receptive and thankful cunt.

My orgasms, as Jenna had promised, were explosive, serial and deeply satisfying.

And as I was coming, my evil little mind was exulting: "You're next, Girlfriend. It's now going to be my turn now to be the top!"

By having strapped the cuffs to her own wrists and ankles, Jenna had signaled that she now was playing the part of the submissive bottom and had yielded the mantle of top to me.

All I had to do was say "spread-eagle" to her and she splayed herself out on the sheets making herself immediately into my sex slave.

In a trice I had her bound to the headboard and the footboard. But, unlike the hanging position she had hauled my legs onto when I was in her position, I had her stretched tight to the sheets below.

While she waited expectantly to see what I would do next, I got out of bed and went over to the dresser.

I rummaged through Jenna's toys in the bottom drawer to see what objects might amuse me.

A ball gag caught my eye.

I'd seen a gag like this at the T4T store and figured out easily enough how it was designed to keep its victim from shouting or complaining. Jenna had gagged me in the morning with the O-ring. And had worn that penis-gag when she'd done me in that very bed. What fun it would be to see how she liked this little number in *her* mouth.

The object I had in hand was a silicone ball with a diameter of about two inches. A leather strap passed through its center.

I brought the gag to the bed and showed it to Jenna. She groaned.

"Before you put that thing into my mouth," she cautioned. "You need to be aware of the safety precautions always adhered to with gags like that."

I was all ears. I was not unaware that there might be some dangers involved.

"In BDSM," she went on, "**Safewords**" are used. That is, the partners agree on a word or sound that definitely means distress. With a gag like the one you have in hand, three grunts in rapid succession mean 'I'm in danger.' A ball gag makes you drool massively which can cause suffocation on occasion if your throat gets stopped up.

"If I go like this…(*grunt…grunt…grunt…*)get that ball out of my mouth fast."

I understood, and was made somewhat uncomfortable imagining that what I was about to inflict on my girlfriend could be dangerous.

The concept of "safeword" made all kinds of sense to me. I knew that I would always insist on safewords from then on, whenever I was involved in BDSM whether I was top or bottom.

"Got it, Girl," I told Jenna. "If you make that sound this ball will be out of your mouth immediately."

She smiled sweetly.

"Great, then," she yielded. "Bring it on."

I placed the ball in her wide-open mouth, behind her teeth. She lifted her head then in compliance, so I could strap the gizmo on.

Now that I had my sub gagged and under my complete control, it was time to have myself some real fun.

I thought I had it in me to learn to be a domina, and, hopefully, even a dominatrix.

Here was my first good opportunity to try out the role.

With my slave stretched out luxuriously on the bed, her lovely body at my disposal, I was perplexed where to begin my assault.

If I was to take my first step on the road to becoming a domina, I felt that I must be decisive, not dithering.

Tits!

There the world came bursting into my mind.

Humiliation!

Aha! Another key word.

My experience at the hands of Headmaster McCarthy, and then of the crew of the good ship *Submissive Miss,* with the follow-up of my encounters with Alex Allen, Zachary Lund and Salesman Cary, I had been provided with enough experience to serve an apprenticeship to the career I had recently set for myself.

Add to all that the games Jenna had taught me to play and I felt adequate to assume the role before me.

Inflict pain.   Pain equals pleasure.   Humiliate your victim. Humiliation leads to joy. Subjugate. Subjugation yields gratitude.

Those guideposts would do for a beginning.

Inflict pain:

I reached down onto Jenna's tits, took a nipple between the thumb and index finger of each of my hands and gave a light squeeze.

What a feeling of power and elation I felt as those nubs burst forth into crimson protrusions.

What a pleasure it was to hear her gasp to the extent she could behind her gag as I gave those nipples a sharp twist.

Humiliate your victim:

"You love that, Slut, don't you?" I sneered. "You're nothing but a common whore after all."

I loved being on the insulting end for a change. I'd never dared put anyone down before. I liked it.

Subjugate:

"You're helpless, Cunt. My slave to do with however I want. Blink your fucking eyes three times to show me you agree that I am your mistress."

Jenna did not blink.

I slapped her hard across the face and saw her blush with pain. Good.

I raised my hand to follow up. Before I could give her another blow she blinked the three times.

She had subjugated herself to be totally mine. Oh, the feeling of power!

The three actions I had just taken produced a euphoria in me such as I had never experienced before.

I knew deep within my very core what I was destined to become.

It might take a lot of pain, humiliation and subjugation on my part from both men and women who were practicing doms and dominas. But I vowed to persist until I had reached the summit of the pyramid.

At the end of the road I was pursuing, I knew I would be a dominatrix.

"Oh, look how happy those titties are from just a little abuse," I exulted. "Let me kiss them for you."

I perceived Jenna's body relax.

I bent over her breasts and sucked and suckled her left nipple.

She purred.

I bent over again, pressing my lips to the other nipple. I inhaled it deep into my mouth and then, unexpectedly, gave it a sharp bite.

Not enough to draw blood. But enough of a nip to cause her cry of pain to dissolve within her gagged mouth.

"Let's see what your cunt has to say about that little bite, shall we, Bitch?" I asked.

I slid down to get a good look and feel at her pussy.

"Well lookie here, Miss Piss Pot," I observed as I ran a lewd hand up and down her slit. "The drab is all wet down here. It seems she relishes pain.

"I wonder, since she's so happy to have her nipples bitten, how she'll feel about having a nice sharp bite to her clit."

When I said that, Jenna's body emitted a spasm.

I lifted her clit hood to gaze at what the sailors on the *Submissive Miss* called "the boy in he boat."

Apt description.

The laddie was certainly looking perky. But I knew I could arouse that clit more with some sweet mouth music.

I began by licking it lasciviously. Up and down. Back and forth. Slurping and drooling all over it.

The little darling grew proudly into quite a tall fellow.

But I knew a good sucking would make it pebble up nice and hard.

And all the time my subject was wondering when I would follow through with my threat and promise to bestow a bite on that most sensitive of spots on the female body.

Keep her on the edge.

"Are you ready to get a love bite there on that pulsating clit yet, you smutty strumpet?" I asked with a wicked leer. "You want it now, don't you? The pain would fill your crotch with your juices and make you exult, wouldn't it?

"But you don't get that pleasure-pain yet, My Dear. It'll happen when you least expect it."

From the way she wiggled her ass I could tell she was relieved and disappointed at the same time.

What a ball I was having.

"Maybe what you'd like is a good old fashioned finger fuck. You fluff yourself off all the time, don't you, you nympho?

"You'd probably rather have someone like me do it for you, wouldn't you, instead of stroking yourself, you lazy slut. Hump the air with your ass two times to admit you're a perverted lesbo who wants a female like me to finger fuck you."

She complied.

Oh, what fun!

Now that I was in charge, I could do anything I wanted to do with my sub. And what had I just decided I would do? Fuck her!

And why not? All I had to do was follow wherever my fancies led me.

I ran the index finger of my right hand up and down her captive slit.

Ooo! Lots and lots of smooth, fragrant juice.

I held my moistened finger up to my nose. Hmmm. Nice.

I put my finger in my mouth. Hmmm. Tasty.

I coated my finger again at the cunt-well.

I held the finger up to my sub's nose.

"Inhale, you perverted slut. Enjoy your own special perfume," I teased.

Jenna took a deep breath. With the ball gag in her mouth I can't say that I could really discern a smile. But I knew there had to be one there.

"Sorry you can't suck the taste off my finger," I chuckled. "But I know you fluff off many times a day like the nasty little pervert you are. And I'll bet you lick your fingers while you're about it.

"Nod your head if I'm right."

Damned if she didn't nod enthusiastically.

That somehow filled me with satisfaction.

I moistened that right hand finger down there again while slathering my own juices on my left index finger. God knows I was slushy enough in my kooze to lubricate my finger to a fare-thee-well. I slid my right finger up and down, up and down, in and out of Jenna's fuck channel.

At the same time I was pleasing myself stroke by stroke in my own treasure house.

The contented sounds in Jenna's throat were testament to her pleasure. And I had barely even begun yet.

I wasn't sure about Jenna, but I knew that I needed a second finger up my own hole. And fucking myself, I found, was much more sensual when I was simultaneously fucking my sub. So she got the double finger up and down, in and out, to the same depths and the same rhythm I was giving myself.

I could tell from the sexy gurgles in her throat that she was responding to being screwed by my fingers with deep satisfaction. But I knew I was getting double her pleasure by fucking her as I was getting self-fucked.

I needed a third finger inside me, so, of course, Jenna was going to benefit by a three-finger fuck.

Ooo! It felt sooo good. I was squirming. She was squirming. I was approaching orgasm and so was she.

I couldn't let it happen to her yet.

So I stopped the operation just short of climax.

"You are so close to coming, Tart, that you're shaking all over," I told her. "But before you do, I have that special treat I promised you.

"So I'm removing that gag…."

She raised her head again so I could unbuckle the gag and get the ball out of her mouth. The slobber that accompanied the ball spilled all over her face.

The relief that she felt at having that ball removed from her mouth was very obvious.

"Now, Slave," I continued. "It would not be right for you to come before your domina, would it?"

"No, Mistress," she agreed.

"So, since your hands are not free to diddle my clit and bring me off, I guess you'd like to use your fucking tongue to do it, wouldn't you?"

"I would love to suck your clit, Ma'am," she agreed.

I climbed up her body with my knees straddling her until my pussy was suspended just above her mouth. I descended on her, pulled up my clit hood and yielded myself to her mouth.

Damn! That girl was *good*! She had me off and flying in less than thirty seconds.

My cry of exaltation reverberated off the walls.

"Now, Tramp," I told her. "It's your turn to come."

I scurried backward on my knees, got my head buried down into her fragrant crotch and my mouth around her clit. I licked, slurped and…

Bit!

"Yow!" she bellowed.

And she came all over my face.

I released her from her bonds and we both laughed and laughed and laughed.

That was as much domination as I needed to experience for then. But oh, what an experience it had been!

CHAPTER NINE

Beating the Boys

Our days in West Hollywood passed by very pleasantly as Jenna and I awaited our departure for Catalina.

We started each day with my deep-throat training.

Jenna kept four sizes of dildos in her treasure chest, S, M, L and XL. She had started off getting me comfortable with Size S[1]. It did not take me long to learn to swallow that tiny pisser while breathing comfortably. Then, size by size she trained me up to XL[2] by the time we were set to leave our beloved cozy room at Motel Defoe. With that giant ersatz dong in my throat I became a virtuoso at erotic gagging while breathing without panic.

Bring those well-hung bastards on!

The day before our departure and my "oral examination" Alex telephoned us. Jenna answered the call with the phone on speaker mode.

"Hello, Jenna…Are you two girls ready to leave for camp tomorrow? …Great! Zack and I are, too…We're planning to come by your place tomorrow to pick you girls up and take you out to breakfast…Seven o'clock… Be sure to be ready…After breakfast we'll bring you back to your room for Colleen's examination…Yes, both Zack and I will provide our members for her pleasure…Ha, ha, ha, separately of course…We couldn't possibly both get in there together at the same time…We certainly hope you have prepared Colleen sufficiently…You know, if she does not accommodate us deeply there will be consequences…May I say *severe* consequences for both of you…Until tomorrow then…Give Colleen our regards…Goodbye."

I was primed for the test. The next day could not come soon enough for me.

Sure enough, the next morning at precisely seven o'clock there was a knock on the door.

It was Alex.

---

1   4 ½ X ¾ inches.
2   9 X 3 inches.

When he entered the room he noticed that I had left my O-gag out on the table very conspicuously. He smiled his wry smile in recognition of the test to come.

He kissed us each and led us to Zack's Beamer parked out on the boulevard.

Zack got out of the car, gave us each a kiss and held the car door open for us to get in the back seat.

We were off for breakfast at the Hollywood Roosevelt Hotel Coffee Shop.

Jenna and I had taken the bus up to Hollywood Boulevard a couple of times during our stay in West Hollywood. And we'd gone into the Hollywood Roosevelt lobby to look around and all. But we hadn't stopped by the coffee shop so that was a treat.

Zack and Alex were good breakfast companions. Zack told us some funny stories about some of the stars and producers he knew. And Alex encouraged Jenna and me to talk about our stay in town.

You would not have thought, seeing the four of us having a pleasant breakfast there, that the two suave gentlemen would be shoving their pricks down my throat after we'd finished our meal.

Or would you?

How would I have known then what was normal for Hollywood?

I was thoroughly enjoying myself. I was looking forward to my test. Instead of those cold dildos I'd been swallowing for a week, I would be having a couple of warm live penises inserted into my receptacle. And I would have lovely gooey jism shooting into my gullet.

So much more rewarding than the plastic objects that had only minor appeal to my sensibilities.

And then, after getting deep-throated, I knew I'd be heading out for that boat trip I'd been looking forward to ever since I was hired.

A real red-letter day.

When we got back to our room after breakfast, all four of us removed our clothing.

My hands were cuffed together behind my back. Jenna's hands were cuffed to the trapeze bar.

Zack removed a cat-o'-nine-tails from his trunk and handed a leather strap to Alex.

It left little to the imagination to surmise what the consequences to Jenna and me would be if my performance failed to please our two masters.

But I was not intimidated. I knew the two men would not be disappointed in my performance.

Zack pointed to a spot on the floor. I did not need to be told what was expected of me. I dutifully went down on my knees exactly where he pointed.

He had me facing in such a way that Jenna would have a full view of my ordeal. Alex stood next to her holding his leather strap in readiness should my performance be less than gratifying.

Both men were sporting handsome hardons. I could see that Zack was, indeed, an XL. I began to drool prematurely in anticipation of the pleasure of entertaining that magnificent pizzle in my gagging throat.

Since I had tasted Alex back in New York there was no surprise in that quarter. His prick, I thought, was nicely sized for my dessert after satisfying Zack.

Zack fastened the O-ring into my already drooling mouth. After a week of wearing the damned thing every morning I accommodated the device very well.

Zack fisted his massive dong and gave it a few gentle jerks to prime it for entry through the O.

Kneeling with my hands shackled behind me I kept my wondering eyes tightly focused on that peter of his as my master approached me slowly, step by step, stroking his engorged rod, his hanging balls swaying from side to side as he moved.

Just as I was poised to receive his member into my mouth, Alex stepped behind me and slipped a blindfold over my head.

It was a surprise, but Jenna had coached me with and without hoodwinks, so I was not alarmed. I had learned that when I was enveloped in darkness I could devote myself to the pleasurable task more thoroughly than when I was distracted by sight.

The crown of his dick slipped past the ring that held my mouth wide open. The warm, pink, velvety head was pulsating as it made its entrance into my salivating yap. The musky scent of horny male permeated my senses. I was already exhilarated.

Blindfolded but unperturbed, I bent my head down onto the welcome pole. I had learned, by Jenna's careful coaching, to respond to the phallus, but to allow the top to take the lead. It was my function to enhance, but never to take any initiative in the process.

My mouth cavity was swimming with my own spit so I knew Zack was enjoying the warm bath his dick was receiving on its entry. My excess saliva was drooling plentifully down my chin, dribbling down over my tits and pooling on the floor below me.

Zack was in no hurry. The effect of my soft loving tongue licking his piss-hole and circling his glans held him spellbound in a welcoming embrace.

When his dome's lips got within my tongue's reach I gave such loving swaths to that most delicate portion of the male anatomy that he could not repress a series of satisfied sighs.

Even within all that saliva in my mouth I was able to sense the intrusion of a tiny pearl of pre-come. I was concerned that Zack might shoot his wad before he had intruded past my uvula into my throat. That, of course, simply would not do.

I consoled myself with the thought that the man had his cock sucked many times, and had pleasure-gagged myriad throats long ere this adventure with me. He surely knew what he was doing.

As that massive dick hit the entry to my throat my erotic gagging began. I concentrated on breathing through my nose, inhaling the distinctive scent emanating from his balls which were batting against my spit-soaked chin.

Oh bliss!

The entrance to my throat had been prepped for a week to receive the velvety bulb that I knew had changed color from pink to scarlet by this time.

Gulp!

I swallowed that throbbing glans and pleasured it with gasping pulsating gags.

It did not take more than several seconds for my deep-throat action to suck out a massive gush of salty, chestnut-flavored jism from his balls as his prick expanded and then reflexively subsided, popping that peckerhead back out of my throat in a bound.

I knew I had performed with star quality as I heard my master scream with elation.

He was thoughtful enough to rip the blindfold off me as he grabbed his shriveling dong.

I was dribbling spit and jism all over the place.

Alex dropped the strap he was holding and rushed over to me, releasing my gag so I could regain control of my swallowing and breathing.

While Alex was taking care of me, Zack settled into a chair, panting furiously, his entire body flushed.

I looked over to see how Jenna was dealing with the scene as she hung there helplessly from the trapeze bar.

Her entire body was wracked with laughter.

I had clearly passed Part One of my oral examination.

Alex was helping me to my feet. And once standing, he removed my handcuffs.

"I think you'd best rest for a while before you take me on," he said gently.

"The Hell you say," Zack managed to mutter. "The girl has done her bit for the day. When she gets to Catalina, she'll be at your beck and call.

"She and I can both use a break now for the rest of the day."

Alex could not suppress a look of disappointment at that bit of news.

But Jenna came to the rescue.

She hung there gazing at Alex's throbbing boner.

"I need to give some deep head after what I've been witnessing," she smiled.

"May I relieve your dire need with my mouth and throat, Master?" she begged Alex.

"With pleasure, you lovely slave," Alex replied as he sashayed over to relieve her from her bondage to the trapeze bar.

So our morning's activities ended with Zack remaining in his chair with me on his lap as he pleasured my aroused nipples and as we both watched Jenna give Alex a deep-throat blow job that left all four of us in fine spirits.

Zack and Alex dressed and left our room telling us to be ready to be picked up by an SUV that would arrive at three o'clock to take us to San Pedro where the boat to Catalina would be expecting us.

Zack mentioned that the supplies he had ordered for me were available at the T4T store.

He told me:

"Cary will see that your supplies are delivered to the boat before it leaves for Avalon. But if you'd like to go to the store later this morning and get acquainted with the equipment, Cary will be happy to show it to you and explain anything you want to know."

When the two men closed the room door on themselves, Jenna and I made a beeline for the bed.

We each had the same urgent need.

We had to get our rocks off after having done the same for our masters.

But once we'd masturbated ourselves and each other, we wanted to get over to T4T to take a peek at the goodies Zack had bought for me.

So we hopped a bus, and when we entered the door of the boutique we were greeted by a grinning and leering Cary.

He effusively kissed us each on the cheek.

"Oh, Darlings," he gushed. "I have such a boxful of goodies to show you. That gorgeous Zack bought toys for Colleen to play with on Catalina that could just make a person practically come on the spot.

"I'll send the box down to San Pedro in an hour or so. But you can take any of the items with you when you leave the store, Colleen.

"Jenna and I can help you pick out any supplies you might find useful on short notice."

He could hardly wait to open the box and show us all the treasures inside.

I was overcome by the magnitude of the contents.

Among the items he pointed out were: whips, paddles, canes, three kinds of cuffs, collars, leashes, three sizes of dildos, a strap-on dildo, a dildo harness, nipple clips, tethers, body harnesses, several kinds of gags, blindfolds, lubes, butt-plugs, vibrators, spreader bars, rope, chains, masks...

You get the idea.

Cary pulled the bullwhip and the cat-o'-nine tails out of the box.

"Girls," he enthused. "I told Perry about you two loves. I have known about Jenna's expertise with the cat for some time now.

"And, as you two darling girls know, I was just thrilled to death when I saw and felt how fabulously Colleen flicks the bullwhip.

"Well! Perry just about shit his panties with excitement when I went on and on about you two. And he made me promise on my mother's honor that if you two dropped in here before sailing off into the sunset, I'd ask you to *do* us."

Jenna and I looked stunned.

First off, who was Perry?

And secondly, what did he mean by 'do us?'

What Cary explained was that Perry was his companion and that they were both masochists (among other things). What they wanted was for Jenna and me to flog them while they were kissing each other and holding each other's dicks.

Something I then knew about myself, and was confident that Jenna shared with me, was the tremendous satisfaction it would give me to *really* whip a man. And whipping two simultaneously would be an even more perfect lark.

Men had always attempted to dominate me – father, headmaster, captain, crew, employer… Here was a human male requesting, but not yet begging, me and my girlfriend to beat him and his boyfriend mercilessly.

What a rush that gave me.

I looked at Jenna. She winked at me.

"Look, Cary," she replied haughtily. "We don't have time to wait around for your friend Perry to get his ass over here.

"Some other time, perhaps."

She clearly knew which way the wind was blowing because Cary rushed to the door to the back room and shouted:

"Perry! Get in here quick. They'll do it for us."

Harkening to the call, the most handsome, strapping hunk of masculinity I'd ever laid eyes on burst into the room.

You've heard of "tall, dark and handsome?" Add buff and bulging at the crotch and you've got Perry.

He smiled a jaw-dropping smile at us and asked, "Will you really?" in a whining voice.

"Down on your fucking knees, both of you," Jenna ordered.

They were on their knees with their hands held in supplication in a trice.

"Crawl over here and kiss our feet," she ordered.

When the two hunks crawled on their knees to where we were standing and kissed each of our feet my crotch flooded.

"Now, Dogs," Jenna demanded. "Beg us to whip your pitiful backs and scrawny asses until they're bloody red."

Perry pleaded, "O Divine Mistresses. My companion and I have been very, very naughty. We deserve severe punishment."

I got into the scene immediately.

Cary was kneeling before me with sad, worried eyes and with his hands clasped again in supplication.

I hauled off and slapped him as hard as I could across this face.

"What do you say to that, you lowlife faggot?" I demanded.

The smile on his face shot bolts of electricity into my crotch.

He gave me the right answer.

"Thank you, Mistress."

I scolded him.

"You will address me as 'Divine Goddess' from now on. Not 'Mistress,'" And I kicked him in the belly, nearly knocking him over.

"Thank you. I will remember that, Divine Goddess," he replied groveling.

I swear. That was the supreme moment of my life up to that point.

"Shall we gag them?" I asked Jenna.

"I would prefer to hear them moan, cry, scream and bellow when we punish them," she replied.

With that settled, Cary asked permission to lock the door to the boutique, which I granted.

We then sent the two submissives into the back room to get buck-ass naked, take the position Cary had requested of kissing and fondling each other, and hold the position until it suited Jenna and me to come in and entertain ourselves by beating the Hell out of them.

When Jenna and I entered the shop's back room, our two submissives were posed together, nude and engaged in a deep kiss while fondling each other's dick.

Their rippling muscled backs and butts were fully exposed for flogging as were their sides.

I whipped my bull over their heads sending a snap that caused them each to jump. But the crack did not cause their lips to part or their hands to lose purchase with the other's peter.

Jenna and I, fully clothed, fell into a kind of dance, a gavotte if you will, around the boys. When I was in perfect position to administer a burning thwack to Cary's back, Jenna was facing Perry's and unfurling her cat at that target. We circled the boys with measured steps slapping welts on their shoulders, sides, butts, thighs, backs and arms.

Although our subservients were forced to break their mouths apart regularly to scream with anguish, their hands never interrupted the mutual masturbation they were engaged in.

My panties were getting soggier and soggier as I inflicted increased pain on our victims. And I knew the tension in my girlfriend's loins matched my own.

At the moment that it was clear that the partners had each simultaneous reached that point where pain morphs into a nearly unbearable pleasure, I, myself, was on the verge of orgasm.

The moans and the screams of the fellows began to burst into bellows of rapture when their pricks began to spurt the elixir from their balls into each other's hand.

And at that precise moment my body was seized with a paroxysm that caused me to drop my whip, reach under my skirt and grab my cunt in ecstasy.

When I saw Jenna drop her whip, I knew that all of us in the room were in sexual Nirvana.

Gary and Perry were lying on the floor in a loving embrace, writhing in a frenzy of painful passion, their bodies a mass of angry welts.

Jenna removed her sopping panties and dropped them on Perry's face. I favored Cary with my own drenched undies.

Each of the boys thanked us and immediately returned to making love to each other.

Jenna and I returned to the showroom.

She picked some tethers, a blindfold, two pairs of Velcro sports cuffs, and a rattan cane out of my box of supplies.

She put the articles in a couple of bags.

"Here, Girl," she said. "Bring these toys with you back to our room. You need to learn how to perform a quickie if the occasion should come up when we get to the island."

I did not know what she was talking about. And I could hardly wait to find out.

We unlocked the door that led out to the street and exited that toy store with smiles bursting from our faces.

A bus returned us two panty-less lassies back to our room at the Motel Defoe.

What a morning we had experienced. You would have thought we would have been exhausted.

Quite the contrary. We were exhilarated.

Jenna had said something about me learning how to turn a quickie. Or something like that.

We were on a roll. I was ready to learn about whatever she had in mind. And she was as anxious as I was to get on with it.

I knew as much as I thought I needed to know about the uses for the blindfold and the rattan cane I'd brought with me back from the store.

Clearly I was at a loss about what the tethers and the sportcuffs were all about.

"These items," Jenna told me, "that we have here constitute your emergency gear.

"Once we get to camp over on Catalina, any fellow staff member, male or female, is free to request to be your submissive, your slave."

I remembered being told that.

The thought was quite titillating.

"How would anyone broach a subject like that?" I asked.

"You know we were all screened for the job on the basis of how we would fit into a BDSM community, Colleen," Jenna scolded. "I've been all over that with you. You know that if you find someone on the staff you want to yield yourself to as a possession, you can do so."

"I already am a slave to Zack and Alex," I responded.

"Of course," Jenna said. "As am I. And every other staff member. But a master may have many slaves. And a slave may have multiple masters. You'll find out that it really does all work out remarkably well when you get to camp."

"Then," I wondered aloud. "What relationship would you say you and I have with each other?"

"That's easy," Jenna smiled. "We are girlfriends, playmates and roommates. We play BDSM games with each other. But neither of us has a permanent submissive obligation to the other.

"We are very likely to still be roommates when we get to Camp Defoe. And I hope we will remain girlfriends and playmates forever."

"Girlfriends and playmates forever!" I echoed. And we laughed and hugged.

"Now, Girlfriend," I inquired. "What's with these toys you had me haul back here to our room?"

"Those constitute your emergency pack," she answered.

"Suppose when you get to Catalina, a staff member comes up to you and asks to be your slave?"

"Male or female?" I asked.

"Either, Silly," Jenna laughed. "What difference does it make?"

"If it's a guy and he's wearing tits it makes quite a difference to him," I joked.

"Do you want to know about a quickie or not?" Jenna admonished.

"Sorry. I couldn't help myself," I apologized.

"Let's say it's a fellow," Jenna went on. "And that he's really cute. And he's kind of bashful. He comes up to you and he asks if you will be his domina. What do you do?"

"If he's that cute, I say, 'Yes, yes, yes,'" I answered honestly.

"Wrong!" she thundered back. "You don't say any such thing. You never accept the submissive's proposal. From the outset he (or she) must accept your exclusive proposal."

"How *do* I respond then?" I asked.

"How did *I* respond when Cary and Perry requested to be flogged by us?"

I remembered her words very distinctly.

"Down on your fucking knees, both of you," I repeated.

"Very good, Colleen," she complemented me. "Then what?"

"Then you ordered, 'Crawl over here and kiss our feet.'" I replied. "Then you made them beg to get whipped."

"You fell into the part of domina immediately, then, too, Colleen," Jenna noted. "That showed you're a natural. You slapped Cary a good one, made him thank you, and ordered him to address you as Divine Goddess. I was so proud of you.

"So if you follow that same pattern if asked, you will be responding to the worm's request correctly."

"Worm?" I questioned.

"Worm, asshole, scumbag…whatever. You have to always, from the very beginning, humiliate, insult, disdain and ridicule a sub or a sub candidate. One of the needs of a sub is to be…well…subjugated. That's his or her need. Your need is to see the candidate as despicable, so you have no qualms about inflicting pain, pain and more pain."

I *loved* it. What Jenna was describing made my nipples and clit perform little joy-dances.

"What then?" I asked.

"Let's act it out," she suggested. "You be the supplicant. I'll be the domina."

"If he's a cute guy, I need a prick to be the supplicant," I objected.

Jenna went to her bottom drawer and took out her dildo strap.

"Here," she ordered. "Put this on and we'll play-act a quickie."

I got out of my clothes in a jiffy and rapidly put on the strap. And, supporting a dick now, I dropped down on my knees.

While I was preparing myself, Jenna had the tethers, the cuffs and the cane set out.

She held up one of the tethers.

"This is a forty-eight inch leather tether," she informed me.

"Using these snaps attached at the each end you can bind a sub to anything that can act as a hook or that can be circled around like a table leg. Bed springs are often handy as attachments. Just look at this room we're in. In addition to all the rings and eyebolts Zack has installed you see the radiator, the dresser, the drapery bar...the opportunities abound. And, I'll teach you how to hogtie a person with a tether when you don't need him to be bound to anything in the room"

"You told me you were going to teach me how to tie a square knot," I complained.

"Don't change the subject, Big Mouth," Jenna snarled, phasing into domina mode. "I'll teach you the God damned knot when we're on the fucking boat. But, since Zack bought you a tether, you probably won't be dealing much with ropes or square knots at camp."

Then she continued menacingly, "Once I get you bound I'll make you sorry for interrupting me."

"I'm sorry, Mistress," I apologized.

"You'll be even sorrier in a few minutes," was her terse reply.

She laid the tether aside and showed me a Velcro sportcuff.

"This is a sportcuff," she explained. "As you see, it's not like a steel, snapping handcuff. It's more like the leather cuffs you've used already. But there are no buckles to hold these babies tight. You just slap them around your sub's wrists or ankles and the Velcro seals them tight.

"These handy items aren't much good for the fun rough-stuff. Because an adept submissive can manage to work himself out of them if he is determined enough."

"You keep saying 'he'," I ventured.

Jenna picked up the rattan cane and told me to face sideways towards the side wall.

She picked up the rattan cane and gave me two good whacks on the ass with it.

Ooo! Rattan hurts so sweet!

"You'll pay for interrupting me again when I have you bound, Smartass," she spat, pointing the tip of the cane ominously at my bare derrière.

"While you're wearing that strap, you're a 'he', Fuckface," she reminded me.

"A 'he' with tits," I jested.

She tried not to laugh, but couldn't restrain the chuckle.

Whack! Whack!

Jesus! She laid into my sore ass with that cane with a fury that I *knew* had to have raised a welt or two.

I decided enough with the wisecracks. I was learning to respect the impact of rattan.

"Hold out your hands," Jenna ordered.

I did so and was amazed at how rapidly she had me manacled.

She handed me the other two cuffs.

"Let's see if you can cuff your own ankles, you clumsy whore," she growled. "And you'd better get it right the first time."

It turned out that the cuffs really were a snap to put on.

Next she brandished the cane at me again.

I thought I had learned everything I needed to know about that cane from the first thwack she'd laid onto me with it.

But this show was hers. So I wasn't going to make any more smartass comments.

"The rattan cane requires a really strong hand and arm to inflict any real chastisement," Jenna told me.

"I guess it's been the traditional spanking instrument of schoolmasters partly for that reason. It hurts and humiliates. It can sting like Hell. But compared with a heavy paddle or with a flogger like a cat or bull, it's pretty puny.

"Yet it does get a sub's attention. And is really the best pain inflicting tool other than your bare hand that there is when training a novice sub.

"As for myself, after about ten hand-administered spanks, my palm isn't capable of delivering any further chastisement at all. So I rely heavily on the cane.

"But even so, in addition to my cat-o'-nine tails my rattan cane is one of the signature pieces of equipment my own slaves know me by."

It turned out that I *had* learned a few things from that little lecture of hers after all.

"Thank you, Domina," I said sincerely.

"Now, you no good, perverted little slut," Jenna snarled. "Let's get you trussed up. Ask me to bind you up tight as a Christmas goose."

"Please bind me up, Mistress," I begged. "As tight as a Christmas turkey."

She let me have a good one with the cane right across my butt.

The tears that flowed from my eyes gave Jenna clear satisfaction.

"Goose!" she reiterated.

"Goose," I managed to repeat through my blubbers.

"If you insist," Jenna replied running the tip of that damned cane between my cheeks and making light contact with my asshole.

My surprised shriek made her laugh despite herself.

"Now," Jenna told me. "I will demonstrate how to use tethers to tie up and tie down a male sub who happens to have luscious tits."

Without further preamble she had me tied up into a docile position with those leather tethers holding me mercilessly tight in a crouch. I could not manage to move my arms or legs while my back and ass were vulnerable to any vengeance my domina might choose to administer.

She slipped the blindfold over my eyes.

In the darkness, even though Jenna was my girlfriend, now, as my domina she was suddenly quite menacing.

"Do you remember interrupting me when I was kind enough to try to teach you about sportcuffs, Bitch?" she asked.

"Yes, Mistress," I answered.

Four nasty whacks with that rattan cane caught my attention. I began to cry.

Coming from out of the dark, the suddenness was quite alarming. And all I could concentrate on was the vibrant stinging sensations.

"What do you say, Pissant?"

"I'm sorry," I blubbered.

"Not the right answer, Bimbo," she responded and administered four blows onto the middle of my exposed back.

What answer did she want?

Another couple of particularly stinging whaps enlivened my brain.

"Thank you, Mistress," I ventured.

"Much better, you despicable turd," she gloated. "Maybe you'll remember to say 'please' and 'thank you' from now on or you'll feel this."

Four sharp blows to my ass that landed on top of the previous welts made me yip.

For some reason, in my hoodwinked darkness an element of fear had intruded itself on my psyche.

"What do you say, Dummy?" Jenna bellowed.

Jesus! I was feeling like a slow learner.

"Thank you, Domina," I hastened to utter.

Two stinging blows on my back that hit right on the spots she'd raised there before.

"'Thank you' for what?" she demanded.

Not fair! She hadn't made me tell her before what I was thanking her for.

While I pondered the correct answer (*Ow!*) another four fierce blows to my aching ass were bestowed.

"Thank you for spanking me for my stupidity," I said.

Jenna untethered me, removed my blindfold and cuffs and let me stretch out and moan.

"Take off the strap," she told me. "I'll put away the cane now. I think you get the idea well enough.

"Now, for the next hour, I'll bind you with these tethers in a dozen different ways. Then you can practice tethering me until you feel comfortable with the techniques."

And so we did, indeed, spend an hour or so working with the tethers.

That hour completed Jenna's teaching. Other than how to tie a square knot, of course.

I had learned enough about using tethers, sportcuffs and rattan canes as bondage restraints and punishment instrument to deal with any novice who might seek my domination.

With the tools and toys Zack had equipped me with, I felt I was ready for whatever might lay ahead when we got to Camp Defoe on Catalina Island.

Bring it on!

CHAPTER TEN

All Aboard

At three o'clock sharp there was a knock on our door. Our bags were packed and we were ready to roll.

Jenna answered the door and a young man simply told us his van was waiting. He did not bother to tell us his name.

We followed him as he carried our bags to the street where a GMC Savanna passenger van was parked. There were six passengers seated inside.

The driver put our luggage in the rear of the vehicle, told us to get in, and away we went.

Jenna knew a couple of the other passengers. They were kitchen staff at the camp whom she knew from the previous year. They were pleasant enough young ladies but Jenna did not know them well enough to maintain much in the way of conversation.

The driver made one more stop in downtown Los Angeles, and a camp counselor of some kind whom Jenna told me she did not know very well got in the van carrying his own suitcase.

From downtown the driver got on what he called the Harbor Freeway and took us to the terminal in San Pedro. Berth 95 was where we were to catch our ferry to Catalina.

We were greeted there by a jolly rotund gentleman named Chip who is a head counselor of some kind at the camp. He showed us where our packages were waiting for us from T4T. Our driver brought in the luggage from the van and put it with our packages.

Somehow Chip arranged to get the luggage for our little group hauled on board, handed us our boarding passes, and before we had time to even get a cup of coffee at the booth in the terminal we were ushered on board and were off for Avalon, the only real town on the island of Catalina.

The ferry ride only took about an hour and a half. During that time Jenna showed me how to tie that knot she'd promised to teach me back when we were in New York.

I don't know what the big deal was. I learned to tie that stupid square knot in about two minutes. Maybe less.

I think Jenna had been holding out on me just to exercise a little superiority over me.

She was my girlfriend. And I really liked her lots. But I have to admit she *did* have a few bitchy qualities.

But then, as you've probably guessed, so do I.

After I had learned to tie the damned knot, we had about an hour and twenty-eight minutes to stand at the rail and watch the flying fish jump out of the Pacific and into the sun-warmed salt air.

It was decidedly a less event-filled voyage than the one I had made on the *Submissive Miss*.

But the prospect of what might be awaiting us at Camp Robinson Crusoe had my panties all bunched up in my crotch.

As we pulled into Avalon Harbor I just loved the setting. The first thing I noticed was the round building they call the Casino that overlooks the blue, blue waters of the bay. The little town that extends from that building gleams white in the blazing sunshine.

I decided that I was going to love this quaint island.

When we debarked, Chip gathered together our Camp Crusoe contingent.

"The next ferry is bringing another bunch of our group here. They won't get here for another hour. Jason will be arriving with the camp's boat a half-hour after that.

"So you guys have an hour-and-a-half free before our boat gets here to take us to Defoe Bay.

"I'll take care of your luggage until the *Happy Peter* gets here. So you can spend the next hour-and-a-half however you want. Just be sure to be back on time to catch our boat or you'll be stranded here in Avalon until someone comes around to pick you up at some ill-defined time.

"And I assure you, you will sorely wish you'd caught the boat with the rest of us if Zack has to send a boat back here for you just because you're late."

"*Happy Peter?* The camp's boat is called the 'Happy Peter?'" I whispered to Jenna.

She answered, "I always thought that was a better name than the *Sorrowful Cunt*."

We both broke out into giggles that attracted the attention of some of the people on the wharf. But we were in a happy mood and did not much care what others thought.

"Come along," Jenna urged me. "Let me show you the town. It's all enclosed within a square mile area so you can get a pretty good sense of Avalon in the hour-and-a-half we have before we have to get back to the wharf."

She led me first to the nearby Casino. It's not a gambling casino but actually a large ballroom and movie house.

Then we went window shopping. There are plenty of hotels, cottages, bed and breakfasts, and restaurants of course. Then all kinds of shops with gift and souvenir stores predominating. But there are clothing stores, beachwear and swimwear boutiques, toy stores, bookstores, coffee shops… Just lots of fun, quaint shops.

I stopped in front of the Island Skin Art Studio. I wondered what kind of art gallery it was.

Jenna nudged me and gave me a sly look.

"It's not an art gallery, Silly. It's a tattoo and body piercing salon."

"This little town does seem to have everything, doesn't it?" I snickered.

"Do you want to get a tattoo or a cup of coffee?" Jenna asked me.

There was a coffee and pastry shop across the street from the Island Skin Art Studio.

And that's where we headed to while away the last half-hour before we were due back at the harbor to catch our boat.

When we got back to the wharf the second batch of Camp Crusoe employees had arrived. Altogether there were a couple of dozen of us who were waiting for the arrival of the good ship *Happy Peter*.

The crowd grew somewhat restless when it was clear that the boat was not going to arrive to pick us up at the scheduled time.

The day was pleasant enough. And the scene that sprawled around us was gorgeous. But still, the crowd was getting a bit cranky at having to stand around with nothing to do when we were supposed to be on board and on our way to camp.

The longer we waited the more slowly time crept by.

When Chip spied the boat heaving into view, he exclaimed loudly enough for all of us to hear, "Jason is thirty-three minutes late."

His tone did not indicate any pleasure in the degree of tardiness.

The boat pulled up to the quay. The lad at the helm manipulated it against the wharf as a second young man jumped onto shore and moored the vessel with hawsers, and secured a gangplank for us to enter the craft.

While we passengers boarded, the two youths busied themselves getting our luggage gathered and stored on board.

When we were all aboard, Chip announced:

"Shipmates, Campers. For those of you who don't know him, this young man here who kept us waiting for over a half an hour is Jason Carlton. The other fellow, who probably isn't to blame for the delay, is his helper, Andy Crawford.

"I think Jason has a little something he wants to say to us before we head for camp."

Jason stood up on a housing to address us.

I had known the name since Jenna had taken me to get my swimsuit at the store in West Hollywood. I had learned then that I would be working with a male swimming instructor and water sports coach.

The clerk said this Jason was "just darling" and that I would "like him."

She also showed me an example of the swimsuit he would be wearing when on duty.

Picturing a buff young man in that suit had given my pussy a buzz at the time.

Now, seeing the handsome youth in person made my pussy lips smack with glee.

He *was* gorgeous.

The poor fellow was nervous and apologetic. He told us how sorry he was to have kept us all waiting and that it was all his fault. He'd lost touch with the time and the boat wasn't in the state of readiness it should have been in…

His apology was rather disjointed and not completely coherent.

Jenna nudged me.

"Not bad, eh?"

"Dreamboat!" I replied.

I decided on the spot that if Jason Carlton made any move on me whatever, I would find a way to teach him to submit and make him mine.

All the way, as the boat sailed along the Catalina coast, I kept my eyes on Jason's trim ass as he stood at the helm and guided us all to Defoe Bay.

But I also made it a point to slyly watch Jenna.

Her eyes were definitely not on Jason. They followed the other lad, Andy, whenever he appeared on deck.

Hmm! A romance she hadn't told me about?

As the boat rounded the headland and proceeded into Defoe Bay everyone on deck waved. The camp came into view and it was breathtaking.

There was a cluster of tents to house the kids who would be coming for their vacation. The tents were large enough to sleep a dozen campers. There was a permanent structure, gleaming white, that turned out to be the messhall and gymnasium for the campers. A slope rose up from the sandy plain and at the foot of that slope was a very attractive, Spanish style building. Jenna pointed it out to me.

"That's the Manor," she told me. "It's the camp headquarters and the staff residence. And lots more."

The 'lots more' had me intrigued. But I decided not to ask about that at the time.

Off in the distance Eagle's Nest Summit rises into the clear deep blue sky.

The site is absolutely breathtaking.

On shore there is a wharf, a boathouse, a pier and a dock. That was the area where I would be working with the kids.

This was the most idyllic spot I had seen in my entire life. And I was thrilled to know I would be living there for the entire summer and would be an active part of the scene.

When Jason and Andy had docked the boat and we were crossing the gangplank onto the quay I saw that Zack and Alex were on shore to greet us with welcoming smiles.

Once we were all off the boat the two men gathered us together to address us.

Three strapping young men swooped onto the boat and hauled our luggage and a bunch of supplies off to the staff quarters.

All of us new arrivals at camp gathered around Zack and Alex.

Our two bosses were all full of smiles and bonhomie. Each gave a short welcoming speech.

At the end of the orations, Zack said:

"Those of you who are returning staff members may proceed on to your quarters at the Manor. Your luggage will be in your rooms when you get there.

"Lunch will be served in the diningroom for the next hour or so.

"When you're finished unpacking and settling into your quarters, feel free to go get yourselves some lunch."

The returning staff headed off towards the Manor.

Jenna, even though a returning staff member, remained behind with us newbies.

"I'll stick by your side while Zack does his orientation thing," she told me."

I told her I appreciated that.

Zack and Alex led us to the building and took us on a guided tour.

It included a large modern dormitory that housed two to a room.

We were shown our room assignments. As expected, I was assigned to be Jenna's roommate.

We looked in the diningroom which was spacious and attractive. There was a library and a well-equipped gymnasium. All very nice.

But the final room Zack and Alex showed us was designated as the Dungeon.

I had seen a few torture chambers in my young life.

There was Headmaster McCarthy's Chamber. Captain O'Sullivan's Chapel was my next experience in such a room. That was followed by the back room of the T4T and the outfitting of Jenna's and my room at the Motel Defoe.

But nothing prepared me for the Dungeon.

Because of my previous exposure, I recognized the spanking benches, hanging crosses, pulleys, rings, torture racks and truss tables. And along the wall was a very full armory of floggers, paddles and canes.

With pride, Zack drew aside a curtain that concealed the entire western wall.

"And here," he announced, "is the voyeurs' loge. Sometimes chastisement of a staff member is handled in private. More often it resembles a spectator sport.

"When Alex or I deem a punishment appropriate for public viewing, we open the curtain and any of you may enter the loge, take a seat and witness the procedure.

"And, of course, it is always the option for any dom or domina on the staff to leave the curtain open or closed while subjecting a sub to discipline.

"You were all inconvenienced by Jason Carlton's failure to arrive with the *Happy Peter* at Avalon Harbor earlier today. His punishment will be executed here in The Dungeon commencing precisely at one-twenty-five. It is only fair that any of you who were victims of his ineptitude should be free to witness the physical payment he will make for such carelessness."

I whispered to Jenna, "I'll be here. I wouldn't miss *that* show for anything in the world."

She smiled knowingly back at me.

Zack continued on:

"I have not yet decided whether Jason's assistant, Andy Crawford, shares any part of the guilt. If I determine that he is culpable in any way, Jason's punishment will be accompanied by appropriate castigation for Andrew. A double-header, so to speak."

Jenna nudged me.

"Nothing could keep me away," she said with a suppressed giggle.

I could tell the girl was really smitten.

"If you choose to attend the session," Alex went on to say, "Be sure to enter by the loge door back there. Do *not* come through the Dungeon.

"An interruption of the proceedings will be dealt with harshly."

Zack looked over at Alex, clearly inviting him to come in with his address to us.

"Thank you, Zack," Alex began. "I believe that summarizes matters new members of the staff need to know about our internal discipline.

"It is imperative for you all to fully realize, though, that what happens in the Manor stays in the Manor.

"The campers who come to our camp are not privy to the disciplinary procedures of the staff.

"Many of their parents are either Zack's or my clients in Hollywood or New York. And because they trust us, they are confident their children will enjoy a thoroughly innocent camp experience here on Catalina this summer.

"You may not all realize the rich programs that we provide for these children. The programs are expensive to run and the parents are willing to expend lavishly for their children to benefit from our offerings.

"Among the programs we provide for our campers are snorkeling, scuba diving, kayaking, canoeing, fishing, sailing, windsurfing, hiking, camping out, nature study, star gazing, camping overnight at Isthmus Two Harbors Campground, glass bottom boat, photography, and arts and crafts.

"Many of you are counselors who will direct these exciting programs.

"We welcome you to our midst. We know you will be a credit to Camp Robinson Crusoe and will provide our campers with joyful experiences they will treasure for the rest of their lives.

"Now, if any of you have individual questions, Zack and I will remain here for a while to answer your concerns.

"You are dismissed to check out your rooms, rest, explore the facilities, go to the dining room or down to the beach.

"For those of you who are interested, remember that the discipline sessions with Jason, and possibly with Andy, will take place here at exactly one twenty-five."

In other words, we were dismissed.

Jenna and I hastened off to our room to unpack and settle in.

Our room was delightful. The first thing I noticed was that we had a four-poster double bed, quite similar to the one we shared in West Hollywood.

And, yes, it had eyebolts on the posts at all the convenient spots.

The room was not festooned, however, with ceiling pulleys, or a hanging cross or eyebolts on the walls.

The furniture was adequate and comfortable. There was a bathroom with a showerhead in the tub.

And we had a nice view of Eagles Nest Summit out our window.

We unpacked and put our clothes away in the closet and the dresser.

"Do you want to go to the diningroom and get something to eat?" Jenna asked me. "Or would you rather look around a bit before we get to watch Jason get punished?"

I told her the coffee and pastry we got back in Avalon had pretty well satisfied me.

"Let's stop by the diningroom anyway," Jenna suggested. "I'd like a bite more to eat. We can pick up a quick sandwich and coffee to go. And we can munch and sip as we explore the Manor. I want you at least to get a good look at the gym and the library before we go see the show in the Dungeon."

I agreed. And off we went.

We dropped by the diningroom. There were a few staff members in there sitting at the tables eating and talking. We waved at them as Jenna went directly to the serving window and rang a bell.

A jolly, plumpish red-faced man came to the kitchen window and smiled at us.

"Gerry," Jenna said to him. "This is Colleen, the new girls' water sports counselor. She's my good friend. She's Irish, so she'll love anything you feed her."

I blushed as Gerry winked at me to show he knew Jenna was just putting me on.

"All we want is a sandwich and a coffee to go," Jenna continued. "Can you get that for us?"

Gerry thrust his hand through the window to shake my hand.

"Nice to have you aboard, Colleen," he smiled. "And what your friend Jenna doesn't know is that we Irish are the most discriminating gourmets on the Good Lord's green earth."

I told him it was a pleasure to meet him.

"I just happen to have some nice corned beef on hand and can put together a couple of quick sandwiches for you girls. Pour yourselves a couple of coffees over there at the urn, and I'll have your sandwiches prepared in a jiffy."

Less than five minutes later, sandwiches and coffees in hand, Jenna and I were out in the halls heading for the gym.

It was not very much like the gymnasium at Ballycormac. There was no swimming pool, of course. The whole Pacific Ocean was only a short walk away.

It was mainly a large room with a number of machines in it. There were both men and women in gym clothes using the machines for body building purposes.

I had never seen such contraptions before. But I recognized that they served in place of barbells and dumbbells. Something I had not previously been into. We did not linger.

Jenna then led me to the staff library.

It was a room well stocked with books.

I was never a great reader and told Jenna so

"Neither am I," she told me "But there's one book here I think you will want to read if any copies are left on the shelves."

We passed sections of shelves marked General Fiction, Classics, Seamanship, Health… and so on until we came to a section marked BDSM.

It was a well-filled category with what I guessed were over a hundred titles.

This was a subject I felt I wanted to master. I decided I might just become somewhat of a reader during my stay on Catalina.

Jenna was looking over the titles. It was clear she was searching for the book she had said would be of interest to me.

"Here it is," she exulted as she pulled a book from the stacks.

She handed me a leather-bound book entitled *The Art and Practice of Female Domination.* The author's name imprinted on the spine was Dominique Tremaine.

"This is a rather rare book," Jenna told me. "It's a private printing of an English translation from the French. As you can see, there are five copies here of the French original. They are quite available. There are only two copies of the English translation in this library. You should check this one out. Unless you read French. I suppose the original may be even better than the translation."

Jenna could see by the expression on my face that I do not read, write or speak French. Although I have a pretty good grasp of the Gaelic.

I kept the book in hand as Jenna led me to the librarian's desk and introduced me to a pleasant young lady there named Penny.

I was introduced to her. She was the librarian. She pulled up a staff roster on the computer screen at her station, found my name and checked the BDSM book out to me.

By then, it was one o'clock.

We had twenty-five minutes to kill before Jason's (and perhaps Andy's) punishment would take place in the dungeon.

We returned to our room where I cuddled up in one of our chairs to skim my library book while Jenna fussed around re-arranging her clothes and supplies in the closet and chest of drawers.

Jenna was right. That book she'd led me to seemed to have everything I would ever need to know in it to become a true top domina. And, with practice, even perhaps a dominatrix.

I skimmed rather rapidly and then began to read in earnest in the first chapter when Jenna alerted me that we had better get ourselves to the Dungeon. We knew that arriving late would not be a good option.

We entered the Dungeon through a door labeled Loges.

The curtain was drawn open so the entire torture chamber was visible from the seats.

About ten people had already arrived to witness the proceedings.

Jenna and I got seats in the first of the two rows.

By one-twenty-five about thirty spectators were seated. Many, or perhaps most, of them had been fellow passengers with us on the boat to Defoe Bay.

At precisely one-twenty-five Zack and Alex entered the Dungeon with nubbed switches in hand. They each were naked except for leather body harnesses that emphasized their sublime pectoral and abdominal muscles.

A kind of leather codpiece covered their genitals, but their sculpted glutes were on magnificent display.

Jason was led into the room on a leash attached to a leather collar about his neck. He was fully attired in the same outfit he had worn aboard the boat.

He crawled along behind his master on his hands and knees, clearly ill at ease at the end of his leash.

Andy's entrance was identical to his buddy's. He was clothed, collared, leashed, and wore an expression at least as doleful as Jason's.

I sprang goosebumps at the sight.

I looked at my girlfriend and saw that her skin was responding like mine.

(And I was pretty sure her koozie was getting as damp as mine, too.)

Voyeurism turned out to be an even bigger turn-on than I had ever dreamed.

I was so pleased for Jenna that Andy had been found to be at least partly responsible for the delay of the *Happy Peter* arriving at Avalon to pick us up. It was clear she was romantically interested in him. So, like me, she was looking forward to her beau getting humiliated and whipped.

The lads were keenly aware that they were being observed by us spectators at the western wall. Although neither of them dared cast a glance in our direction. The point of them being brought into the room collared, leashed and on all fours was to make their humiliation more bitter for being observed by their friends, acquaintances, and co-workers.

Zack and Alex led their charges directly in front of where Jenna and I were sitting. I suspect they were not unaware that some kind of chemistry existed between the lads and us.

Zack gave the first order to the two miscreants.

"Roll over!"

And, as a pair of well-trained dogs would do, the two subs did roll over.

Alex's order followed.

"Play dead!"

Neither Jenna nor I could suppress our giggles when we saw our dreamboats roll over on their backs, fold up their arms and legs, and close their eyes.

After all, the effect really was comical, you know.

It was the next command that had to be the most mortifying to the boys.

Zack simply ordered:

"Sit up on your haunches, face the audience and put your paws together and look repentant!"

As they took that lugubrious position, Jason's eyes made contact with mine and Andy's eyes met Jenna's.

Oh, how we wished we could control our reactions. But, alas, we could not and the laughter showed in our faces. The boys' mournful expressions were testimony to the fact that we had added to their humiliation.

While they maintained that stupid pose, Alex gave the next direction to them.

"You have been negligent, thoughtless, selfish slobs. Bark once if you agree."

Their bark was, to say the least, tepid.

They each received a smart blow on the back with the nubbly switches their masers wielded.

"Louder!" the doms shouted in unison.

The laddies belted out raucous barks.

Zack demanded, "If you would like to receive ten strokes more as a down payment on the punishment to come, bark twice."

The sounds from the dog-boys was resounding this time.

"Without touching the floor with your hands, turn your backs to the loges," Alex demanded.

Supported by their bent legs only, the act of turning around was ludicrous. I was nearly ashamed to find it so humorous.

But I was shaking with laughter. And so was Jenna.

"You have been bad creatures," Zack told the boys. "Bad animals must learn the consequences for their actions. So, without rising off your knees, remove the clothing from your torsos, fold the articles neatly and set them to your side."

Off came their shirts and undershirts.

Both boys had the torsos of muscled athletes. Enough to make a girl's twat twinge.

"Prepare for ten applications of the switch to your backs, Curs," Zack intoned. "And as you feel the sting, each time, you are to say 'Bow wow.'"The words were scarcely out of Zack's mouth when the two men slashed fiercely across the subs' back with the switches.

"Bow-wow."

What a silly thing to have to say. And how amusing.

There were ten applications in all. Each left either a red mark or a nasty welt. We were honored on-lookers and connoisseurs of the patterns as they developed on our favorite boy's tender skin.

The "bow-wows" were emitted with increasingly painful sounding whimpers, sobs, cries and howls. By the application of the tenth thrashing it was impossible to make out the words "bow-wow" that were being uttered.

My panties were absolutely drenched by the spectacle. I had just witnessed as erotic a sight as I had ever beheld. And I doubted that was the end of the show.

Zack had used the words "down payment." That suggested that we would be privileged to witness more humiliation and more physical pain.

"Get up off these ridiculous positions like men, you dirty dogs," Alex commanded. "You see the red bordered rectangle on the floor before you. Trot over there mincingly, face each other, and wait for us to proceed with the next frolic."

The red rectangle was some fifteen yards deeper into The Dungeon.

The young men were on their feet immediately. And they did trot rather winsomely to the designated spot and faced each other. The tears that had flowed from their whipping were still quite visible on their faces.

The masters left the boys standing in the center of the room staring at each other's tear-stained face.

"Remove your shoes and socks and place them neatly outside the red rectangle. Now!" Zack demanded.

Jason and Andy promptly sat on the floor, removed the objects, fastidiously placed them outside the zone and were very soon standing facing each other as previously.

Alex issued the next order:

"I want you to remove each other's belt and place it next to the appropriate shoes and socks."

The operation was more awkward than one would imagine, but was accomplished without too much delay.

"Very clumsily done, you dolts," Zack complained. "We expect our counselors to be more adept. Show us you can do better at removing each other's trousers. Andrew, you unbutton and unzip Jason's pants and lower them so he can step free of them."

To give him credit, Andy, though clearly ruffled and nervous, did what I thought was a creditable job.

Jason was next told to remove Andy's pants. And did not receive any criticism from the masters when he had accomplished it.

Both boys were now standing in their boxer shorts. I was looking to see if either had a boner. Each of them was too disquieted and preoccupied to have the power of erection.

The next order given was for them to remove each other's undershorts.

This was not accomplished well at all.

The two lads, as I later learned, were just a year older than Jenna and me. That is to say, they were nineteen.

At that age apparently many boys, and certainly these two, are still sensitive about showing any interest at all in another male's genitals. Zack and Alex were playing against a taboo that even transcends the teen years.

Jason and Alex were blushing, perspiring and mortified.

I thought the humiliation of removing each other's boxers must be the height of psychological sadism.

I was wrong. More was coming.

"Look at these two pansies," Zack addressed the audience. "Neither can so much as spring a decent hardon to show his masculinity. All right, boys. Take your boyfriend's pecker in hand and manipulate it into a nice hardon for the benefit of your audience. You may fill your palms with saliva if you think a bit of natural lubrication will help do the trick."

I wasn't sure either boy, even at the vibrant sexual age he had attained, could overcome the psychological barrier facing him.

But, again, I was wrong. It was not long before the audience had a view of two bright red peckerheads aimed at the ceiling.

A few in the audience applauded.

That was too mean for even Jenna and me to do.

At that time we had not yet reached the necessary level of sadism we have each now grown into.

"That's enough of your perversions, boys," Alex said. "Drop each other's dick. It's time to get on with the physical punishment you each asked for."

So that was, indeed, the end of the mind torture phase of the boys' punishment.

I was ready to now observe the flogging I knew would follow. And I am pretty sure Jenna was anxious to see the laddies get it as well.

The floggings were quite routine. There are six wooden crosses in the Dungeon. The boys were attached to two of the Roman crosses, with their feet extended on a lower crossbar that gave no support. Thus, they hung spread-eagle and uncomfortable.

Zack wielded a bullwhip while Alex exercised his cat-o'-nine-tails. Jenna and I were aware of our masters' individual preferences in floggers so there were no surprises there.

As the guys hung painfully suspended on their crosses, their backs presented exquisite targets not only to the doms but also to Jenna, me and any others in the audience who happened to be sadists.

"How many minutes late were you in arriving at Avalon Harbor to pick up our staff members?" Zack asked.

I knew the question was directed at Jason since he was the man at the helm.

Jason replied loud and firmly, "Thirty-three minutes, Sir."

Alex shouted, "You! Andrew! Wasn't there any way at all that you could have reminded your playmate of his responsibility to our waiting staff?"

"I could have insisted we leave on time, Sir. I was as remiss as Jason."

"Then do you merit as many strokes as that vile procrastinator, Jason Carlton?" Alex asked.

"Yes, Sir," Andy answered manfully. "I do."

Zack clearly addressed them both when he spoke next.

"You previously asked for ten strokes of the switch as a down payment on your punishment. Now, if you deserve thirty-three lashes total for your dereliction of duty, and we chalk up credit for your down payment, how many remaining strokes are you asking Alex and me to inflict on your bare backs as earned chastisement?"

"Twenty three lashes, Sir," both the young men sang out in unison.

Zack and Alex did not allow the matter to stand there. They made each boy beg, wheedle and implore a master to flog him twenty three times.

After sufficient pleading, the men agreed to administer the desired strokes.

The snapping sound of Zack's bullwhip as it wreaked its sharp, stinging, agonizing pain across Jason's rippling muscled back played raging sensations within me from my nipples to my clit.

Each stroke caused my nipples to harden, my clit to throb and my mound to moisten.

By the tenth lash, I was in a passionate agony needing orgasmic relief.

I was delighted with myself that I had come to this show braless and pantyless.

I slipped my left hand under my loose blouse and allowed my thumb to brush a yearning nipple. A sideways glance informed me that Andy's punishment was having the same effect under the blouse of my girlfriend sitting next to me.

I pinched the tip of my nipple and felt the blood pound there. I knew it was possible that others in the observing crowd might be aware of what my antic left hand was doing. I felt fairly sure they were too engaged in enjoying the whippings at the crosses to be looking in my direction. But if such was not the case, I was too sexually worked up to care about it in the least.

The pulsing at my crotch demanded attention when my inner consciousness had counted the fifteenth snap of the bull. Without disengaging the entertainment I was providing my left tit, my right hand, which was resting on my right thigh, began a gradual creep towards Heaven.

Finger by finger, inch by inch, my hand continued its inexorable climb snatch-wise. My left hand grew more excited as it became aware of the ascent of its partner up my crotch so my left thumb and index finger pinched, pulled and twisted my nipple painfully enough to cause tears to form in my eyes.

Oh how sweet it was to be aware that no dratted panties would hinder the release I was desperate to discharge down below. Because my right index finger had unerringly discovered my slit and was favoring it with soft, satisfying massages along the labia.

The twentieth snap of the whip triggered my right thumb to give succor to my throbbing clit as its neighboring three fingers made entry into my cunt.

I could tell that Jenna was trembling with the same frissons that were overwhelming me.

The last twenty-three blows struck the backs of our heroes.

Jason's piercing scream spoke more of ecstasy than of agony. If there is a sound that expresses ecstatic agony, that was what my dreamboat shouted with timber-shaking volume.

His buddy's howl blended with it in a sensual duet.

While Jenna and I each felt it necessary to constrain our own vocal expressions of rapture as we came convulsively just as the boys' ordeal terminated.

Jason and Andy were released from their crosses of anguish and delight. Each fell to the floor, unable at first to stand.

As the audience left the loges, the curtain was drawn. The punished subs were left to their own devices unobserved. And Jenna and I returned to our room.

I started to read my book in bed as soon as I disrobed and laid myself down onto the covers. Then Jenna snuggled up to me and pressed her naked tits against my bare skin.

It turned out that our orgasms in the loges were not enough to subdue the passions we had experienced in The Dungeon.

So we each satisfied our self and our companion in multiple acts of love until we fell asleep exhausted.

CHAPTER ELEVEN

Learning the Ropes

On Saturday morning at ten o'clock the *Happy Peter* hove into Defoe Bay laden with the first batch of kids. Jason was at the helm. Andy was second in command. And the boat was arriving exactly on time. Of course.

The passengers were as delightful a bunch of boys and girls as you could imagine. The anticipation of the camp experience ahead showed clearly on those bright young faces

Life outside the Manor was a universe distinct from the world within.

As much as I loved the lifestyle in the Manor, permeated always by the shadows of BDSM, I resonated as well to my life as girls' water sports counselor.

I loved that job. It even surpassed the pleasure I had felt teaching at Ballycormac.

Part of the job was teaching swimming to the girls who did not know how. Most of the girls came from homes that had swimming pools and whose social life included pool parties. But there were some who needed instruction and it was a pleasure to give them the skills and thrills of swimming.

The water sports of course included swimming races of various kinds. And water games like Marco Polo, which always elicits as many laughs as splashes.

And I developed two water polo teams, each of which, under my direction, became quite effective competitors.

Jason was working with the boys, of course, in Defoe Bay, often near my activities but just as often at some distance away.

I approached him with the idea of matches of my girls against his boys. It was something that had not been attempted before at Camp Robinson Crusoe, but he was game.

We organized races, relays and water polo matches of girls versus boys. My girls did very well, sometimes, at first, to the embarrassment of the boys.

But Jason and I both worked with our charges to teach them both good sportsmanship and the folly of sexism.

This worked to my advantage in the pursuit of my prime goal – the winning of Jason Carlton into my affection and, more important, into my domination.

For, as you know, Jason *was* my pet project.

Catalina Island is twenty-two miles long and, at its widest point, eight miles across. So it has nearly forty-five miles of coastline. At many of its bays and inlets there are summer camps run by youth organizations or by entrepreneurs like Zachary Lund.

I went to Zack to broach the idea of an inter-mural program with other camps on the island. He was favorably inclined towards the idea. He was in contact with the managers of most of the other youth camps and contacted those he knew best by cell phone.

There were four other camps that showed interest in participating in an inter-mural water polo league.

Zack told me he thought that if we were to initiate an inter-camp league it should be for boys teams as well as for girls. But to make it easier for Jason and me to work together, he wanted to introduce the concept to Jason as his own idea rather than mine. I could not agree more.

He called Jason and me into his office and presented the idea to the two of us. Jason and I showed genuine enthusiasm.

Zack scheduled Jason and me to visit the water sports counselors at each of the four camps that had shown interest the very next Saturday evening. Jason would pilot the *Happy Peter* to the sites of the other camps.

Had establishing an inter-camp league been the real reason lurking in my mind when I proposed the idea of an inter-camp program?

Was it even a part of Zachary Lund's secret interest to see what would happen when the girl he had early spotted as a potential domina would have romantic access to a boy who had shown himself clearly to be a latent submissive? Those were conspiracy theories I tried to keep hidden in the darker recesses of my sexually sadistic inner soul.

Our meeting with Zack had been on a Wednesday. That gave me three days to fantasize about an evening on board the *Happy Peter* with Jason on the romantic Pacific under a seductive moon.

On Wednesday, Thursday and Friday nights I fantasized aloud, abetted by Jenna's lascivious interruptions, as we luxuriated in our mutual masturbations in our lovely double bed.

On Saturday, Gerry the cook prepared a picnic basket for Jason and me to take on our cruise to the camps.

I was stoked. My project was about to get underway.

Jason and I met at the boat. I wore a loose blouse, a short black skirt and tennis shoes. He wore a blue sweatshirt emblazoned Camp Robinson Crusoe, white shorts and deck shoes.

He looked so cute I nearly hugged him on the spot.

There would be time enough for that later.

When we boarded the *Happy Peter,* Jason appeared somewhat nervous. Even flustered.

I was all a-tingle. Nervous was pretty much the way I wanted my quarry to be.

I got on board with my basket. Jason unmoored the boat, hopped aboard and headed us out of our harbor.

It was a beautiful moonlit night. The sea was calm and my hormones were buzzing.

I sat next to Jason as he piloted the boat.

We headed northeast along the coast towards the Isthmus.

I opened the picnic basket.

"Look!" I exclaimed. "That mischievous Gerry included a bottle of wine and an opener in the basket. Do you ever drink wine?"

Jason, with a sheepish smile, admitted that he did.

As we approached the first cove northwest of Defoe Bay, Jason pulled in and dropped anchor.

"Why don't we check out what all Gerry packed for our dinner?" he asked.

"Besides the wine?" I teased.

"Besides the wine," he agreed.

There was an assortment of sandwiches, some fruit, and, to accompany the bottle of wine, only one wine glass.

Was Gerry thoughtless or thoughtful?

Jason uncorked the bottle and poured the wine in the glass as I unwrapped a couple of egg salad sandwiches.

He handed me the glass and I took a sip.

I passed the glass back to him. He made somewhat of a show of sipping so his lips touched the glass exactly where there was an imprint of my lipstick.

Hmm. Good sign.

As we munched our sandwiches and tasted our wine, Jason glanced at me somewhat moon-eyed and said. "I saw you sitting in the loges the other night when I was getting punished for being late in picking up your group in Avalon."

I licked my lips more suggestively than was needed to clean them of egg salad.

"Was that the first time you've ever been punished?" I asked.

He hesitated. Then he smiled shyly (and deliciously, I might add).

"No," he admitted. "I've been punished before."

"What were you punished for before?" I urged.

"Because I have often been a bad boy," he admitted.

A long silence ensued during which we passed the wine glass back and forth, partaking of more libation.

"We'd better get on to that first camp we're supposed to visit," I suggested.

We put our sandwiches back in the basket and proceeded to Camp Marvista.

After we had met with the Marvista counselors and discussed dates and venues, we headed for the next camp. But, before getting there, Jason pulled into an uninhabited inlet and dropped anchor for another "bite and a sip."

"Have you been a bad boy recently?" I asked him between nibbles and swallows.

"Oh, yes," he smirked. "I have had very wicked thoughts, Colleen."

"We'd better press on," I suggested.

So we deferred further discussion of his wickedness for a while.

I was sitting next to him to the right as he steered the boat towards Camp Baden Powell. A dolphin poked his head out of the sea to our left.

"Look!" I enthused. "A dolphin."

As I did so, I 'inadvertently' grabbed his bare left thigh.

He jumped and shivered, but was cool.

"Yeah," he stuttered. "Cute little fellow, isn't he?"

I left my hand on his thigh and glanced at his crotch.

The 'cute little fellow' I noticed was not a dolphin in the sea but a Jason's darling cock in his pants struggling up against his fly.

Jason made a shy attempt to touch my thigh, but I brushed his hand away.

Never let a potential submissive take control.

Before we pulled into the dock at Camp Powell, Jason idled the boat and I removed my warm hand from his goose-pimpled thigh. He needed time to calm down before meeting our next hosts. It would not do for him to disembark sporting a hardon.

After our successful meeting with the Powell staff, we sailed on towards Crystal Bay where the next camp was located.

But before we got there, Jason anchored the boat for a "refreshment stop."

I won't say we had been over-indulging at the wine bottle. After all, we had not yet consumed a third of the bottle between us. But I also cannot claim that the alcohol had not affected us in the least. That would be overstating the case.

I asked him directly, "Do you feel a need for a little spanking?"

He did not answer, but shyly nodded his head in affirmation.

"You bad boy," I admonished. "You know what you have been doing wrong. You have had filthy thoughts, haven't you?"

He dropped his eyes and looked sheepish.

"And when you've let yourself think such thoughts, you've touched yourself. Admit it to me."

My reading of Madame Tremaine's book had supplied me with some fine quotes to use on potential bottoms. And my prospective sub was clearly falling under the spell of the words I had memorized from the book.

I followed up with precisely the comments the Madame had prescribed:

"You want to get spanked. Don't you, Jason?"

A very soft, hesitant "yes" ensued.

That was my clue to quite firmly and authoritatively command, "Drop your pants and get yourself over my lap...Now!"

Jason looked startled. He didn't quite expect that. He tried to struggle with some shred of internal resistance.

"I said 'Now!'" I reiterated.

And damned if that gorgeous young man didn't stand up, unbuckle his belt, drop his short pants and stand somewhat equivocally to my right side.

I placed my hand on his back and pressed. With a small amount of reticence he let me drape him over my lap, his underwear and butt in the air, his rock hard peter pressed against my mound and his hands braced on the deck to my left.

Triumph!

I placed my hand gently on his right bun.

I rubbed it and kneaded it. I felt his hard prick dance against my cunt as I massaged his ass.

Then I lifted my hand and...*whack!*

Boy, did he ever jump.

Left bun. Kneading. Hand raised. Hold the position so he couldn't know when the next smack would land...*smack!*

Damned if the dreamboat wasn't blubbering. And his dong did a dance as he arched, sank and dry fucked my crotch with each spank I administered.

I had had fun before. But this beat all. (No pun.)

After I had tanned his hide ten times I ordered him off my lap as I scolded him with each whap for his evil thoughts and his admitted jacking off in the past.

He was aroused. I was aroused. But I needed to save the best to happen later. I had not memorized Madame Tremaine's book for nothing.

I ordered Jason to get his pants back on and get us to our responsibilities at Crystal Bay.

At Crystal Bay Camp, I was amused to see how gingerly Jason sat on his chair at the discussion table. Our hosts could not know that his bottom was red and tender. But I was so aware I could not control the moisture gathered at my Y.

And, speaking of Y, when we had finished our discussions with the folks at Crystal Bay we headed off for our last stop, the YMCA Camp at Palm Cove.

Jason wanted to drop anchor before we got there but I told him that was not a good idea. Although we had hit the wine bottle sparingly, and I was sure we had not jeopardized our mission by appearing tipsy up until then, Jason's red face was beginning to match his red bottom. And I suspected that, in the case of his face, the wine had contributed to the pink tint.

When we concluded our last discussion at the YMCA camp, we headed back down the island's coast towards Camp Crusoe.

Jason wanted to drop anchor several times. But I told him to sail on and on until we reached that cove we'd first stopped at after we had left our camp. It was there that I planned to net the big fish I was angling for – Jason Carlton.

Although Jason had wanted to drop anchor at several spots along our way back to camp, as we approached the cove I had mentioned, his determination to pause seemed to wilt as he steered the boat into the cove.

"Maybe we had better get back to camp before it gets too late," he stammered.

I believe he had been turning matters over in his mind as our evening together was drawing to an end. He had exposed a part of himself to me that apparently had lain for years in a shadow of his soul.

He had admitted to me that he had wanted to get spanked. He had submitted to a rather vigorous spanking administered on his underpants-clad rump. He knew that if we stopped at this point I would make him expose his bare ass to my punishing hand.

For Jason, this concern about doing so was weighing increasingly heavily on his mind.

Firmness, Girl. Firmness.

"Drop anchor here," I demanded in no uncertain terms.

That was what he needed. For he obeyed my order with what I interpreted as a sigh of relief.

When the *Happy Peter* was stabilized in the cove, I sternly told him to sit down on the deck at my feet.

He did so. I noted a trace of fear in his eyes. He was on the brink of a submission about which he seemed to waver.

"Look me in the eye," I commanded.

I was sitting on a chair. He was sitting several feet below me so he had to look up to make eye contact. I was in the power seat. He was the obeisant.

"You have freely admitted to me that you feel a need for punishment for your thoughts and actions, haven't you?" I asked.

He nodded.

"Tell me that you agree, Jason."

"I agree, Colleen," he said forthrightly.

His body relaxed. He was responding well to his position vis-à-vis my own.

"Before we get back to camp, deep down inside you want me to give a good spanking to your bare bottom. Don't you?"

He nodded his head.

I was concerned that I might lose him at this point if I insisted on his uttering his assent. The best course would be to let him act out upon my commands.

"Stand up, Jason," I demanded.

He arose immediately. The bulge in his shorts was testimony to me that he was mine. His penis now demanded fulfillment.

My own snatch had grown equally insistent.

"Remove your sweater," I ordered.

Good. He had no undershirt beneath it. His muscular upper body sent shivers from my breasts to my mound.

"Stand at attention in front of me, Jason."

He responded immediately.

I reached forward, unbuckled his belt, unbuttoned the top button of his shorts and unzipped his fly zipper.

He remained in place but began to tremble. But he did not resist. He wanted what was going to happen. The throbbing of his erect pecker spoke that unerring truth.

I gave a downward pull to his shorts and they dropped onto the deck.

The machinations of the erection behind his boxer shorts might have been an embarrassment to the boy. But the urgings that had his balls in an uproar trumped any embarrassment. The trick now was to get the underpants over that raging prick without causing any discomfort to him.

I very gently and carefully got the elastic band pulled well away from his ripped abs, over his peckerhead and let them slither down to meet his short pants on the deck.

I stood before him and pulled my panties down so they rested, like his underwear, limp on the deck.

The delighted look in his eyes was tonic to my soul.

It was time for me to apply a lifetime's learning about spanking to Jason's ass. I had learned the techniques I intended to apply, not from books or lectures, but from being the one whose butt had been reddened by masters.

"Reach down and pick up my panties," I directed him.

"Give them to me," I said simply.

With my panties in hand I bade him turn his back to me and hold them there. I tied his wrists together with those panties knowing that degree of bondage would increase his feeling of helplessness and subjugation.

At our stop before going on to Crystal Bay, I had broken Jason of any resistance to draping himself over my lap. And he'd experienced the salacious tremors falling just short of ejaculation as he dry-humped my cunt as I tanned his ass when we were there

Now we were here, in a new setting. And as a preliminary to his submission to me, I pulled up my skirt as he leaned himself across my lap so his bare boner would sit athwart my exposed cunt. Unlike the previous spanking he had received, this time his bare skin would be rubbing against my naked mound. So that when I began to spank his cute ass and he arched up and down in response, he would be getting a delightful dry hump.

And so would I.

Now I was ready to apply the lessons I had learned from my own submissive past as spank*ee* rather than as spank*or*.

My first smack down on my victim's bun would not be a heavy-handed slap with the flat palm of my hand. That kind of smack, I'd learned, does not really hurt that much.

But when there's a quick rebound to the blow, a bounce if you will, the effect is a sharp, biting sting.

So I practiced putting the bounce on my blows to the lad's ass. Left cheek, bounce. Right cheek, bounce. First one, then the other cheek, with a memorable rhythm where expectations of the spankee are part of the experience. The spanking is like a dance at this level. And that part of the session lasted for ten slaps to each of his moons.

The tango the fellow's cock was playing on my pussy was causing his pecker to launch itself up into a blue woodie. And the juices accumulating at my vulva were lubricating his shaft more and more as his humping became less and less dry.

The pain of the slaps meshed for him with his sexual exhilaration, so that pleasure and pain were fusing into that new sensation known only to devoted masochists.

Jason's sobs and shouts from the hurt merged with the sound of rapture heard accompanying his intense sexual excitement.

The next thing I wanted to practice on Jason's backsides was a different spanking technique.

Somewhat before Daddy had left our home to go to Mullinahone to play house with Mrs. Dugan he had developed a new spanking technique which he applied to my ass in his continuous dedication to "teach me a lesson."

Well, I had learned a lesson from him all right. One that I would now apply to the darling blushing ass draped across my lap.

It took me a while, back when Daddy changed his technique, to figure out what he was doing that made the stinging suddenly more painful. What he had stumbled on was a way to make the spank more psychologically painful. I was not, at that time, sophisticated enough to recognize that "psychological pain" was even a concept.

What Daddy had done was introduce a sound element into the procedure. That element which I later learned separates the milder chastisement of a cat-o'-nine-tails to the more sinister punishment of the *snap*, was the sound that accompanies the sting of a bullwhip.

That sharp sound explained the difference between that flat tone that Engineer Aiden elicited from his bongo drum and the exciting, sensuous beats that First Mate Bates drew from the skin of his drum back on the *Submissive Miss*.

I realized that what Daddy had incorporated into his spanking protocol at the end of his stay at home was the flicking of his wrist during his hand's descent and landing with his thumb and fingers rather than with a stiff wrist and the palm of the hand.

The snapping sound of that technique burrows right into the center of your being to cause a pain that has no name.

Applying the bongo technique to Jason's rosy ass introduced a much more emotional tone to his yelps, sobs and cries. The mix of pain and exultation in his moans was making my pussy so damp that I was in as aroused a state as my victim.

But I was determined to raise the level of his simultaneous agony and delight further still. I did so by roughly massaging the painful blush on his butt at the precise moment when he unclenched his crack to relax it again.

That is not to say that I limited my slaps to his buns. I applied an occasional whack to the tender skin of his thighs or to the base of the hillocks.

One of the important lessons I had learned from being a spank*ee* was that if you are not sure where the next thwack will land, your mind feels an additional element of fright along with the pain.

As Jason made vain attempts to stifle his sobs and screams, sexual tension built up within him (and within me as well). He blubbered and screamed "enough." Then he screamed insane shouts of "more, more, more" as he orgasmed with the wildest yelp yet.

His orgasm was simultaneous with mine. As he ejaculated, I reached between my legs, grabbed his balls and gave them a gentle squeeze. My action caused him to buck right off my lap and writhe on the deck as he spurted his seed all over the place.

When he ceased coming and flip-flopping all around I reached down and untied his hands.

Madame Tremaine's basic precept for the dominatrix is: "You must love your submissive. He must know that you love him enough to care to chastise him for his grievous faults. He must believe that no one else in the world loves him enough to subject him to such pain and humiliation."

As Jason continued to wallow prostrate on the deck in a state of sexual euphoria, I addressed him.

"Jason. If I did not care more about you than about anyone else in the world, I would not have exerted myself to give you the release you needed from your suppressed guilt.

"Tell me, Love. Why did I punish you just now?"

"Because you love me," he responded through grateful sobs.

"Exactly so," I told him. "Now, when you are able to pull yourself together and cease wiggling around about the deck, you may get yourself up onto your hands and knees and crawl over here and kiss my foot."

It took the lad a bit of time to calm down enough to control the shudders of rapture that coursed through his lithe body.

When he regained control, he managed to right himself into a hands and knees crawl towards me.

He bent his mouth to my right foot and kissed it passionately, repeating over and over again, "Thank you...thank you...thank you."

Jason was *mine!*

When he pulled himself together and had put his clothes back on (and I had slipped my panties back up), Jason admitted to me, amid winsome blushes and stammers, that he had learned at Camp Crusoe that he "got off" on being a submissive...a bottom...a slave.

At the time he was not able to actually tell me that he wanted to be *my* submissive...*my* bottom...*my* slave.

Nor did I want him to make that declaration yet. Whenever she can manage to work it, the idea should always seem to originate with the top, not the bottom. The domina should set the tone. The submissive should then beg to be accepted.

I had ingested the basic rules very well from Madame Tremaine's Bible.

"You not only enjoy bondage, domination, submission and punishment, Jason," I informed him. "Deep down you really need it to atone for the wicked wretch you are. Don't you?"

The young man assented with a nod of his head.

"It is possible that I might be willing to assume the position of accommodating to your need. The little encounters we have just enjoyed aboard the *Happy Peter* were way too brief and impromptu to determine whether you have the necessary qualities or perseverance to make you a good candidate for absolute submission. You would have to undergo much greater humiliation and physical pain to show yourself to be an adequate bottom.

"When we get back to camp, I want you to privately consider whether you can manfully withstand the submission you would have to show me and your other friends and co-workers at the Manor as I abuse you within those walls.

"Naturally, in camp, outside the Manor, our relationship would have to be what is appropriate between any two counselors. No hint of your subservience could be displayed in the presence of the boys and girls at the camp.

"If, after due consideration of what a slave owes his mistress in terms of absolute and unequivocal surrender, you may come to my room tomorrow evening after dinner to show me your sincerity and beg me to be your domina. I care enough, yes, even cherish you enough, to at least consider you as a candidate for submission."

Whew! I thought I had handled that very well indeed.

I did not allow Jason to comment on what I had just said. I told him quite firmly that I desired him to pilot our boat back to Defoe Harbor in silence.

And, with a broad smile on his face, he complied.

It was late at night when *The Happy Peter* hove into port and we disembarked.

Without a word of discussion between us, Jason and I made our way across the camp and to our lodgings in the Manor.

And, although our return home was maintained in silence, I was quite aware of Jason's joyful posture, which indicated that he was very well pleased with the experiences that had befallen him in the course of the evening and night.

When I got to my room, Jenna was sleeping lightly. But when I was preparing to go to bed she stretched, yawned and sat up.

"How did it go?" she asked lethargically.

I told her about my boat trip. About how Jason had come under my dominance on our stops bay by bay and inlet by inlet.

She perked up wide awake during my recital and greeted the news of my progress with the dreamboat with wild enthusiasm.

"He'll come by the room tomorrow evening after dinner, I'm sure," she predicted.

"I wouldn't be surprised," I opined modestly.

We discussed the "quickie" we had enacted together in our room back in West Holywood. Back then, she had bound me with the forty-eight inch leather tether, had blindfolded me, cuffed me with Velcro sportcuffs, and beat me with a rattan cane.

I recalled that learning experience vividly and knew I could use some of it as a base when (not if) Jason came to me after dinner the next day.

It would be simple to add various forms of degradation and embarrassment that I had learned from personal experience and from the Madame. With such knowledge I knew I could bend young Jason Carlton to my will.

The next evening, after dinner, Jenna did not return to the room with me. She said she and Andy Crawford were going to the gym to work out together.

I interpreted that to mean she was going to the gym to work on Andy.

I waited in the room with quiet assurance, knowing that Jason would soon come begging at my door.

I did not have long to wait. The three timid knocks on my door assured me that Jason had come seeking my unquestioned dominance over him. It was up to me to provide the road for him to follow into willing slavery.

When I opened the door, I looked down towards the corridor floor. Because there Jason was, on his knees, holding out a bouquet of flowers towards me.

For my part, I was conspicuously holding my rattan cane in one hand and a bag containing some Velcro cuffs and a blindfold in the other.

I recognized the flowers. They had ornamented the tables in the dining room where the staff had recently been dining.

Essentially they were stolen flowers, presented to me in supplication. Delightfully pathetic. I loved it.

Jason appeared to be about to rise to his feet.

"Stay on your knees, Worm!" I admonished him. "Crawl into this room on your knees and place your offering at my feet. Then in token of submission kiss my foot."

I stepped back a few spaces so he could shuffle up to me holding that pathetic bouquet before him.

He laid the flowers at my feet and kissed my right foot.

"Were you raised in a barn, Pig?" I scoffed. "Get back there and shut that door behind you."

He crawled back on all fours, butted the door with his head, crawled back to me and rose up on his knees like a good doggie.

He had learned the pose back during his penance at the Dungeon just a few days previous. He was *so* cute!

"Before I can even begin to consider you as a subject, I need to appraise your physical being," I told him.

"Stand up and disrobe!"

He had bared his ass to me on the boat. And had actually come on my lap and then exposed himself lewdly as he ejaculated on the deck of the boat.

But I knew that coldly taking off his clothes in front of me now would embarrass him even more so. And he needed to have a great deal of embarrassment heaped upon him to make him a dutiful submissive.

To his credit, Jason removed every stitch of clothing on his body while exposing himself full-frontal. He blushed and shivered. But he obeyed.

I now had ample opportunity to evaluate his equipment. I had become well acquainted with his darling ass on the boat the previous night. And had witnessed his wild ejaculation.

Now, as he stood there bravely before me with his youthful hardon pointing generally heavenward, I could make a cool evaluation of what he had to offer me.

His prick, when measured against the dildos Jenna and I owned, measured somewhere between a small and a medium when in its ithyphallic state (between four-and-a-half by three-fourth inches and five-and-a half by one-and-a-quarter inches.

It had a gentle curve to it which I found fetching.

"Turn around," I ordered him.

When I'd taken a good gander at that butt I adored so much, I had him turn back to face me again.

"You are a bit short in the penis department and your ass is pretty scrawny," I lied to him. "But your pectorals and abdominals have benefited from your swimming. So, overall, physically you are acceptable to be my subject once I get you get branded."

The look on his face when I mentioned branding was an absolute delight. He was horrified and showed it. But I did not deign to explain what I meant by branding yet and let the worst possible interpretation fester in his mind.

"Now," I told him. "We have to see how you relate to bondage and to caning."

I still had my rattan cane and my bag of goodies in hand. He observed the cane almost with longing.

A good sign.

I set the cane and the bag on the room table and with great deliberation removed the cuffs.

"We are at a point here, Jason," I told him. "Where I plan to test your endurance to pain. If you remain in the room, I will bind you and beat you. The caning will be intense and unremitting. Even if you beg me to stop, I will not do so."

Jason looked alarmed at that, as he well should have.

"However, there *is* a way for you to get the process stopped at any time if you feel you are in danger or even if you truly can bear no more pain. The escape hatch is a 'safe word.'"

He smiled. The expression was not totally unknown to him.

"If you remain here for your beating, and at any time you wish me to stop inflicting punishment on you, your safe word is 'Friday.' You know. Robinson Crusoe's man Friday?

"But be aware, Jason. The safe word will not only end our session. It will also end our BDSM relationship forever.

"Do you understand?"

"Yes, Colleen. I do," he answered.

"Do you want me to proceed with the bondage and chastisement?"

"Yes, I do," he declared again.

"What is the safeword?" I asked.

"Friday," he replied.

"Good then," I informed him. "Get back down on your knees and hold out your wrists."

The young man responded with an air of satisfaction that showed me he had come to my room expecting the course I planned to lead him through.

I rapidly slapped the Velcro cuffs around his wrists.

"Now, lie down on the floor on your back," I commanded.

When he was prone on his back I bade him lift his legs into the air so I could strap cuffs to his ankles.

I could tell that he could scarcely smother the glee at being shackled by me.

And, I guessed that the pleasure I felt in assuming so boldly my new role as domina might even be exceeding his own delight at this point.

"Get back on your feet, you lazy oaf," I chided him. "You can't just lie there hoping to escape the pain you know you deserve. Come on, Asshole. Move it!"

Jason bounded to his feet with the grace of the athlete I knew him to be.

There were two easy-chairs in the room, one of which I had claimed as mine. The other was Jenna's by rights.

I had Jason stand at the back of my chair with his feet spread apart.

The feet of the chair were not as wide apart as I would have liked. But they would have to do.

I attached his footcuffs to the chair feet.

"Bend your waist so your head is pointed towards the seat bottom, Dummy!" I growled. "Do you expect me to wait all day for you to assume the position?"

He responded by physically bending himself down so his ass was pointing toward the ceiling in ideal caning mode.

I stepped around to the front of the chair with my blindfold in hand and slipped the hoodwink around his head.

I now had my sub bound and blinded. He was mine. All mine.

"I asked you a question, Jason," I scolded him. "Are you hard of hearing? I asked if you expected me to wait all day for you to assume the position."

"I'm sorry, Colleen," he answered. "No, I do not expect you to have to wait for me."

I swung the cane back and snapped it sharply across his exposed ass. My arm and wrist motion felt just about right. And the red mark

I'd left on his bum gave me a happy lift.

"You are to address me as Colleen only outside the Manor," I told him.

"Within this building you must always affix the term 'Belovèd Domina' at the beginning or end of every statement. Do you understand that, you bad boy?"

I gave him another blow of the cane for emphasis. That one left an even brighter mark on his butt than the first smack.

Yummy!

I could tell I was already getting better in inflicting red slash marks on my sub.

"Ouch! Yes, I understand that, Belovèd Domina," he answered.

I enjoyed the sound of "Ouch!" even more than his sentence of compliance.

And I knew I would get even more soul satisfying sounds of pain and agony out of him before this session was over.

"Hands behind your back," was my next order.

Once his wrists were close together I attached the cuffs together.

Now the lad was helplessly bound and subject to whatever sadistic fancies emerged from the darkest depths of my vengeful soul.

Yes, my vengeful soul.

Because although Madame Tremaine had indicated that a dominatrix has to really love her slaves, I knew there was another element playing in my mind. The resentments I secretly harbored for the unjust indignities various males had heaped upon me since childhood had left me with an urge for revenge against the male sex. And deep down, I knew the reason I wanted to be a domina and then a dominatrix was so I could beat the hell out of the bastards.

Fueled by my love for the boy as well as by my deep-seated resentment and anger at the entire male gender, I proceeded to whip Jason within an inch of his life.

I vented my fury on him as I simultaneously expressed my love. The dual emotions are not antithetical in the least. They consist of a unified sentiment that fires a passion unique to dominas and dominatrices.

That drive allowed me to beat Jason with my rattan cane to a degree just short of what appeared to be his endurance point. I was careful in my aim to leave no marks or welts that would show at the shore when he was in his swimsuit. His suit, as you know, was comprised of a lycra rushguard top and knee-length shorts.

My blows all landed between the top of his butt and the top of his thighs.

That zone was replete with delightfully tender meat for my hungry cane to bite into.

Jason sobbed, moaned, pleaded, and begged. But he did not utter the safe word.

His pecker rode back and forth over the top of the chair. He humped, arched, and wiggled. Finally he emitted an exuberant scream…He came! All over my precious chair.

Since Jason was blindfolded, there had been no reason for me to forbid my left hand from entertaining my crotch while my right flagellated my sub.

Jason had one giant orgasm. And I had seven very satisfactory ones during the session.

With Jason's climax the caning session came to an end.

I removed his hoodwink and cuffs and allowed him to kiss my foot in gratitude for what I had done for him.

I seated myself and told him to get dressed and sit on the floor in front of me. I even gave him permission to make eye contact with me.

I exulted in how gingerly he had to sit on the floor. I knew his ass was on fire. And new tears drenched his cheeks as he squirmed on those flaming buns. But he made no complaint at all.

"Jason," I told him. "You have managed to endure the first test preparatory to being accepted as my slave. I assure you there will be harsher trials ahead for as long as you choose serfdom.

"So I accept you now tentatively as my subject.

"However, our pact of mistress to submissive will not become formal until you are branded as a slave.

"The branding, in this case, does not involve anything as harsh as a red-hot iron. It merely consists of a tattoo."

Jason could not help but look relieved at that news.

"The tattoo is to be inscribed on your pubis. You will need to shave off your pubic hair, of course, to prepare the area for the needle. It used to be customary to have the words 'servus sum,' Latin for 'I am a slave,' to be branded on a sex slave. In these times the single word 'Slave' suffices.

"For as long as you are under servitude to me, you must shave your pubis daily so the branding is not obscured.

"When is the next time you are going to pilot the *Happy Peter* down to Avalon?"

He told me Zack was sending him and Andy to town on Sunday to pick up supplies.

"When you are in town, find the Island Skin Art Studio and get yourself appropriately branded," I ordered him

With that order, I dismissed him.

On the following Sunday evening, after dinner, Jenna made sure to be absent from our room.

I heard three knocks on the door.

I allowed Jason to crawl into the room and kiss my foot.

"Arise and drop your pants and underpants," I ordered.

He complied.

I granted him a smile when I made out the word "SLAVE" tattooed in black and lined in crimson on his pubis. The word was not quite obscured by the bobbing hardon standing proudly before it.

That was the crowning moment of my life up to that time.

CHAPTER TWELVE

Colleen Riley: Dominatrix to the Stars

As the summer progressed Jason became a perfect abject slave. I led him around the Manor on a leash, at times afoot, at others crawling on all fours. His devotion to me was acknowledged and accepted by all members of the staff.

He was scarcely the only person dwelling in our compound who was an open and obvious submissive. After all, Zack and Alex had chosen their staff not only for our expertise in conducting an enjoyable and healthy summer experience for the children who came to Camp Robinson Crusoe. They had additionally chosen us on the basis of their interest in our BDSM potentialities.

Just weeks after Jason got branded, Andy became Jenna's slave and paid a visit to the Island Skin Art Studio. Jenna had him branded with a blue butterfly with her name emblazoned on its left wing. The location for the brand was on Andy's left ass cheek.

In August, as the end of summer vacation was approaching, I began to wonder what the Fall season held in store for me. When our campers left to go back home and start school, what would await me?

Back in New York when Alex had hired me, he told me that after summer camp closed, if I was "compliant with their needs," Zack had contacts who could forge a passport and a "green card" for me so I could work in America without a worry.

As far as I knew, I had been compliant. So I felt reasonably sure that my masters would follow through.

I talked to Jenna about my concerns.

"Don't fret about it," she assured me. "Zack will come through. You can count on it. You'll get the passport and green card all right. And remember how I told you back when we first met that Zack takes care of his people? That once you've proved you've got what it takes he'll get you a job?"

Yes. I remembered all that quite well.

"Just relax," she told me. "He'll be calling you to his office any day now and let you know what he has in mind for you."

I did not have long to wait. I got the summons from the boss the very next week.

I remember it well. It was the third week in August. An envelope was left for me in our room telling me to report to him on Sunday night at seven in the evening.

When I arrived at his office, he greeted me warmly.

"You may well be wondering what awaits you, Colleen, now that our summer camp is about to shut down for the season," he began when I was seated facing him.

"Yes, Zack," I answered. "As you can imagine, I will admit to being curious."

He laughed good naturedly at my response.

"When Alex and I hired you to work here on Catalina Island, we saw a potential in you for a profession beyond that of a water sports counselor. And when Cary, the manager of the T4T boutique in Hollywood informed me of your virtuosity with the bullwhip, we knew we had picked a winner."

A winner? What kind of winner?

"At the time I ordered Cary to set aside a catsuit, boots and a cap for you."

Catsuit, boots, cap? I had seen some of the dominas at the Manor wearing those outfits. And back when we were living at the motel in West Hollywood Jenna had predicted that Zack would buy one of those costumes for me. At the time I was too naïve to even know what she was talking about.

"I have a present for you, Colleen," he smiled. "It's in that a box over there on the table. I'll bet you can guess what it is."

I could guess all right.

I went to the table and opened the box. And what I saw in there disturbed me a bit. For it was a spandex dominatrix costume, catsuit and all.

As I said, I had seen some of the dominas and dominatrices wearing those outfits in the Manor. And frankly, they were a turn-off to me. Particularly when the women walked around in an exaggerated manner carrying their whips ostentatiously.

And here my boss was offering me just such a uniform.

What now?

I realized that my reaction to Zack's gift would have a real impact on whatever he had in mind for me employment-wise.

So I feigned both delight and surprise and rushed over to him to give him a hug and a deep passionate kiss.

He beamed.

"Put them on, Colleen," he laughed. "Let's see how you look as a dominatrix."

I undressed and put on the outfit.

I did not like the feel of the spandex against my body.

There was a cheval mirror in the room. So after posing seductively for Zack I went to view myself.

The reflection I saw was not pleasing to me. But I put a smile of delight on my face and ran back to Zack and gave him an even tighter hug and a deeper kiss than before.

"Sit back down again, Colleen," he told me. "I want to talk to you."

So I sat, anxious to hear what lurked in the future.

"I have kept an eye on you from the very beginning," he began.

"I had hidden cameras in the hotel room in New York where you were interviewed by Alex. And in your motel room in Hollywood. Then on the *Happy Peter* when you showed such expertise in spanking. And, of course, I had cameras in your room here in the Manor where you performed like a well-seasoned professional dominatrix with Jason.

"Let me show you just a few of the pictures I have of you."

He switched on his computer monitor and bade me come around to his side of the desk to see his slide show of my progress from novice to domina.

I have to admit, as I watched those pictures, I was impressed with myself. There was no question that I was a natural.

Zack had assembled about twenty pictures from his collection for my viewing. When he'd run them for me I went back to my chair.

"You can see why I was impressed by you, Colleen, from the very beginning," he told me. "I have an eye for talent of many kinds. I am seldom wrong in my taste. And, in your case, I was right on.

"I would be willing to set you up with your own studio in Hollywood.

"I would be your mentor, although you clearly need very little mentoring. Your innate abilities are obvious.

"I would also be your business manager. And, most important of all, I would be the person who would direct clients to you who have needs for bondage, humiliation and physical punishment."

"Back in Ireland we call such a person a pimp," I thought. But I did not see fit to inform him of that.

Here I was being offered a job as a professional dominatrix in Hollywood. A profession where I could take out my revenge on the male gender as well as express my love for the bastards at the same time. My smile this time was sincere.

"That sounds fine to me, so far, Zack," I enthused. "Tell me more."

"I own a studio on Yucca Street in Hollywood, just a few blocks from the Erotic Museum," he explained. "I can set it up with the kind of apparatus we have here in the Dungeon. And I will supply you with your own apartment in West Hollywood.

"My contacts in the Los Angeles area with actors, musicians, writers and studio executives are truly extensive. Among other enterprises in which I am engaged, I am able to help them find outlets for their libidinal needs. You will never suffer for lack of clients. A large number of artists have a deep need for BDSM ministration.

"In return, you will pay me seventy percent of all revenue that you collect from your profession. That is my due as your mentor, business manager, client resource and benefactor."

So far it sounded like the man was offering me a dream job.

"The profession of dominatrix is not a one person operation, Colleen," he went on. "There are risks involved. It is always possible that a submissive will turn ugly. For that purpose there must always be a backup person on hand.

"Additionally, for many operations an assistant is required to help the dominatrix subject and humiliate the slave. So you will have two assistants at your disposal, a male and a female. I will supply such personnel."

"It sounds to me as if you are offering me a job, Zack," I ventured.

"More than a job, Colleen," he replied. "I am offering you a profession for which you are very aptly qualified."

"May I show you my acceptance and gratitude by sucking your cock, Master?" I asked.

I deep-throated that man's gigantic cock until I had drained every single little sperm-cell from his low-hung balls.

When I left his office, both he and I were well satisfied.

That transaction with Zachary Lund took place five years ago.

I love my studio on Yucca and my spacious apartment in West Hollywood.

After a very successful full year as dominatrix in the catsuit, I put away the traditional costume and attired myself in black peasant blouses, short black leather skirts and spiked heeled sandals with black latex straps that wrapped halfway up my silk-stockinged legs to the knee.

Neither Zack nor Alex, nor any of my clients objected to the change of costume. The outfit reflects who I am far better than the synthetic garb associated with a former BDSM age.

My income more than meets my needs and I am able to send enough money regularly to my mother so she is quite independent. She still lives with her aunt, but shares all expenses now.

Many of my clients are celebrities whose names would be quite familiar to you. In addition to film stars I have other movers and shakers in the industry who need their masochistic needs met by my mastery of the bullwhip and by the humiliation I love to demean them with.

In their lives outside my studio, nearly all my clients control others powerfully.

When they enter my studio, they bear my brand and fall on their knees to kiss my feet.

Life is good, my friends. Life is good.

ABOUT THE AUTHOR

Tim Desmondes

Tim Desmondes and his wife reside in Southern California.

Tim is the author of ten books other than the present volume published by the Nazca Plains Publishing Company:

- *Sex and Loathing in Hollywood*
- *Sexual Diversity and Perversity in California*
- *Dracula Sucks Hollywood Dudes*
- *Venus Does Adonis While Apollo Shags a Tree*
- *Arthur Does Camelot*
- *Whores, Love and Pistols in the Wild West*
- *Robin's Too Tight Tights*
- *Sex and Love in Paris and Frisco*
- *Agnes Sorel: The Breast and Crotch that Changed History*
- *Beowulf, Wulfgar and Their Friggin' Horny Gods*

Desmondes

Sex and Loathing in ...
HOLLYWOOD

SEX AND LOATHING IN HOLLYWOOD

Tim Desmondes

Desmondes

Sexual Diversity and Perversity in California

SEXUAL DIVERSITY AND PERVERSITY IN CALIFORNIA

Tim Desmondes

Desmondes

Dracula Sucks Hollywood Dudes

Dracula Sucks Hollywood Dudes

Tim Desmondes

Desmondes

VENUS DOES ADONIS WHILE APOLLO SHAGS A TREE

Tim Desmondes

Venus Does Adonis while Apollo Shags a Tree

Arthur Does Camelot
a novel by
Tim Desmondes

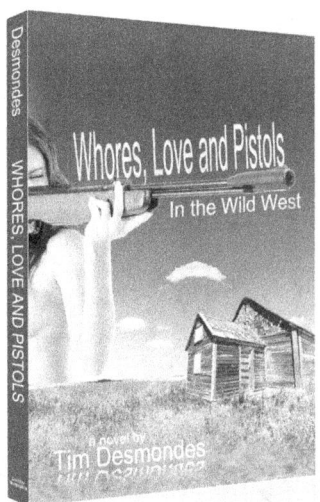

Whores, Love and Pistols
In the Wild West
a novel by
Tim Desmondes

inside
ROBIN'S
too tight tights
a novel by
Tim Desmondes

Sex and Love in Paris and Frisco
Tim Desmondes